Catch Me if I Fall

by

DOMINA ALEXANDRA

2024

Also by Domina Alexandra

I'd love to thank my editor, Julia Wagner. I have enjoyed working with you to make this story a success. And to my Publisher; you saw the vision I had for this story and pushed me one step further.

To the real Sky! Now you can't say I've never done anything for you! Don't read the book in front of me!

Chapter One

Sky Wyman answered the phone on the third ring as she warmed leftovers from last night's dinner in the oven. She'd come home exhausted, most of her day spent around models, working as a makeup artist.

Sky leaned back against the kitchen counter and answered in an exhausted voice, not recognizing the number on the caller I.D.

"Hello."

A woman introduced herself as a nurse and Sky straightened, picturing her brother with tubes down his throat. He had a habit of taking risks and as the nurse spoke, she held her breath. The nurse didn't leave Sky room to speculate further, quickly saying her dad's name.

At the age of sixty-six, Sky's father refused to retire as an electrician and handyman even though he'd had the means to for a while. He could preach about good work ethic all day, but if falling off a ladder didn't make him see the reason to hang up his tool belt, Sky would surely assist in giving him a reality check. The nurse explained his condition and after a few minutes back and forth, Sky hung up the phone and headed to her room to pack a bag. Her father had broken his hip and a rib, and he would need support to make a full recovery.

Her mom had passed a couple years back and despite there being three other siblings who lived within arm's reach of their dad, Sky wasn't naïve enough to believe they'd come and help him right away. As the oldest, that responsibility would automatically fall to her.

Her hometown was a few hours away and if she timed it right, she'd be there by eleven tonight. She sent a text to her friend, Amber, who was also a makeup artist, to cover her upcoming gigs and then sent a group text to her siblings, making sure they were aware of their dad being hospitalized.

Christmas would be in two weeks and Sky wondered if she should clear the rest of her calendar and stay through the New Year. Hopefully by then she'd convince her siblings to take turns sticking by their dad's side.

It took less than an hour to pack and shower and then she was on the road back to the home she'd always had fond memories of. In her car, she called her siblings one by one and eventually listened to an audiobook about the theories of artistries and the understanding of color for the rest of the journey back home.

She managed to arrive at the hospital without disruption, weary and anxious to see her father. The hospital was small, with only five floors of separation to maintain exposure and individual practices. It was the only hospital in town, so it was kept busy.

She checked in and a nurse guided her to her father's room. She was thankful to see him asleep, without any signs of distress. Sky's entire drive was haunted by the image of a tube down his throat, his body visibly damaged, with an agonized look in his eyes. She released a breath, shoulders loosening as she looked around the room; the lights were out with background noise coming from the television. Her father loved falling asleep to crime shows, and an episode of 20/20 was on. The large window that had a view of the main road was partially draped closed.

The nurse left and Sky crept soundlessly into the room to avoid rousing him. There was a cushioned chair beside the bed, and Sky helped herself to it. She sent a quick text to her siblings and then leaned back, staring up at her father. His trimmed hair was mostly gray, and his smooth face had very few aging lines, which helped disguise his true age. He was lean and lived an active lifestyle.

Sky watched his belly extend and relax from each breath. It calmed her, along with the sound of the machine lightly beeping to assure her he was alive. The more she listened and watched him breathe, the more it soothed her as she fell asleep.

*

Sky shifted awkwardly on the chair, her leg arched over the armrest, with a blanket draped over her. Her head slipped off the edge of the chair and she jolted awake. Eyes droopy, Sky straightened lazily and looked up to find her father watching her with a smile on his face. His big brown eyes caused her to stand abruptly and reach over for his hand cradled at his side.

"Dad." There was a nurse in the room, checking his blood pressure, and giving them the illusion of privacy. Sky ran her fingers lightly through his hair and leaned in to kiss him on the forehead. "You should have woken me," Sky chastised.

He tried to laugh but hissed from the pain that jabbed at his ribs. He carefully reached up and brushed his hand along his upper stomach as if that would ease some of the pain.

"Please, do not crack any jokes right now. I need you to get better," Sky said sternly.

He waved one of his hands in surrender.

"I'll behave but I can't promise it will last," he teased.

The nurse chuckled, replacing his I.V fluid bag.

"Has he been acting up since he got here?" Sky asked.

The nurse looked up, winking at her father before answering.

"He's been one of my best patients."

The nurse had clearly become a fan of her dad, her response tainted by his charm.

"Can you at least try not to move around too much?" she supplicated, eyes wide and pleading.

Her dad gave her a cynical look.

"You do know it will be months before I'm… *healed?*" He gestured with his fingers to quote *healed,* and Sky scowled.

"I promise you, for a man of your father's…" the nurse paused when Sky's dad gave her a silly expression. "Statue…" she said with a wide grin. "He is doing excellent. Otherwise, he would have been met with my famous narrowing of the eyes if he were pushing his limits."

"Scary," her dad joked.

Sky rolled her eyes, but the nurse's words relaxed her nervous hovering posture.

"Thank you."

"Of course." Once the nurse was finished, she squeezed Sky's father's arm.

4

"Someone will bring you breakfast, and the doctor will want to run additional tests, so expect more prodding."

Sky nodded her thanks, and the nurse left them alone. She turned toward the window behind her and noticed the sky showing its first signs of daylight. She scooted the chair forward and sat, leaning her elbow into the bed to stay close.

"I have to admit, getting a call that you were in the hospital was almost enough to make me want to move back."

He stared down at his daughter; his expression serious for the first time. He knew not to comment when it regarded the possibility of her moving back, unless he wanted to argue, so he stayed silent. They'd shared several deep discussions on the topic over the years, and Sky had reacted uncomfortably every time.

She loved the town and the memories she had here, but it was too small, and she would never be able to have a real career. Not that she was doing anything extravagant now. But it was still something.

Her father reached over, careful not to move his entire body, and squeezed her hand.

"It will be a long recovery, but I will be fine. It means a great deal, you coming home on such short notice."

Sky grunted. "It was never a question of if I should come. You know that."

He nodded. "I do." He sighed and looked up at the ceiling. "As for your siblings, well... I question them."

For some reason, despite them all growing up in the same house, Sky's siblings seemed to miss out on the meaning of family and what that meant. As the oldest, Sky had seen the beginning stages of her family flourish successfully, her father owning his own electrician and handyman business and her mom working as a beautician and often traveling for shows. But they hadn't started off with money in their pockets. Sky remembered the first ten years of her life, living off canned vegetables, rice, and top ramen, a meal they often ate. By the time her siblings reached a decent age, they'd only known good food, trips, and financial wellbeing. It did teach them how to handle and make money on their own, but they also lacked certain values. Despite the differences she had with her siblings, Sky knew if their father was really in trouble they'd come.

"Jackie said she'd visit in a few days." Sky wanted to bring a smile to his face, and it did.

"You are a great sister." He arched a brow. "And daughter."

Sky smiled and leaned down to kiss the hand that still rested on her own.

His food came, and Sky assisted him so that he wouldn't have to move. Time seemed to flow right by, and it was afternoon when the doctor came in.

"You have the house key with you?" her dad asked.

She arched a brow. "Is that your way of kicking me out?" she joked.

He smiled. "Yes. You need to get some fresh air. Take your stuff to the house, and let the doctor do his job without you micromanaging him."

Sky laughed and stood.

"Fine," she whined playfully. "I'll go, but I will be back later."

Her father grinned. "And sneak in some fries and a burger when you get back."

The doctor narrowed his eyes, a smile on his face.

Sky kissed her dad on the forehead, picked up her purse and walked toward the door, her back stiff from falling asleep on the chair.

"I'll be back by the time *they serve you dinner.*"

He pouted and waved as she left. The nurses and doctors stationed at the center of the emergency room desks were busy on their computers as she walked toward the exit. Sky hoped by the time she returned he'd be tucked away in a comfortable ICU room. When she went outside, the cold breeze cut through her exposed skin and she curled into her coat, moving quickly toward her car parked alongside the hospital entrance. She dug through her coat pocket for the car keys and pressed the alarm to unlock her door. She rushed across the drive-through front entrance, too consumed with escaping the cold to notice ice from the overnight snow.

Sky's arms flew out, her body falling backward as she screeched, anticipating a hard, painful fall. What Sky did not expect was strong arms encasing her like a safety net that caught her before she met the ground. There was a body pressed against her back and Sky managed to straighten before she looked any more helpless. She turned, embarrassed that she had needed rescuing and was met with a woman wearing a black beanie and a Game of Thrones Christmas sweater, small blinking Christmas lights laced through it. She looked Sky's age, early thirties. She was dark skinned, lean, and about an inch shorter than Sky. Her brown eyes scanned over Sky as if searching for injuries and then down at a large blue portfolio she had dropped on the ground.

The woman moved quickly to pick up her portfolio, some papers with drawings sketched on them sticking out.

The ground was wet, and it seeped through one of her drawings, but she didn't seem bothered.

Careful not to slip again, Sky bent down to help, the woman gathering most of them up. Sky tried to get a better look at the woman's art but figured it was not her business to ask.

They both stood, the woman awkwardly avoiding Sky's eyes.

"Are you okay?" she asked.

Sky nodded and frowned. The woman looked familiar, but she couldn't place her. Her town was comparable to a small city, so it was possible she'd never met the woman before, but something itched at the back of her brain. It would be rude to ask, especially if the woman knew her, so Sky decided to not touch the subject of identity, though if she didn't say her name, it would be obvious.

"I'm fine. Thanks. I don't need to be in the hospital too," she joked.

The woman nodded, rubbing the back of her neck, and cradling her portfolio in her other hand.

"Yeah. Mr. Wyman would hate to see his daughter in a hospital bed beside him and especially not for the same reasons." The woman's attempt at a joke was dry but it still managed to bring a smile to Sky's face.

Before Sky responded she mentally chastised herself for not knowing the woman who clearly knew who she was.

"I should get going. I have to drop this off before work. Stay safe…" she pointed at the ground. "And watch the ice."

Sky frowned, bewildered and stuck, struggling to recall who the woman could be, and glanced down at the ice on the ground from the mention of it. Sky watched the woman head into the hospital and gave up on guessing her name, figuring she wouldn't see her again, and got into her car without further incident.

Chapter Two

Eva had nearly lost all composure when she leaped toward the woman parked beside her and caught her midair. She hadn't seen Sky Wyman in almost two years and that had only been at a distance. After the near fall, Eva could tell Sky didn't recognize her, not that she was surprised. Eva had always lived in the background of others and when she'd moved out of the foster care system at eighteen, she'd grown more taciturn, living in solitude right on the border of town.

Sky Wyman and Eva had attended the same schools since the age of ten but never shared more than a few sentences.

Despite the negative experiences Eva suffered, she didn't stay because of the people. It was the culture and the nature that surrounded the town. It was the memories she loved replaying every time she passed specific places.

"What are you doing here?" Denise narrowed one eye; her stethoscope placed around her neck. She wore dark blue scrubs, with her dark coiled hair pulled into a ponytail. She had worked as an emergency room technician for the last four years and was one of the few friends Eva had acquired. Denise was also her ex-girlfriend.

Eva had returned to the emergency room later in the day after the person she'd come to see was unavailable. It was almost five, the waiting room filling up with people with various illnesses and injuries. If she didn't leave here soon, she'd have to come back tomorrow.

"I'm here visiting someone," Eva said, annoyed it was taking so long to go up.

"Come on," Denise waved her to follow. "The nurses down here are too busy and probably forgot to update you. I know who you're here to see."

Relieved to be rescued from the hot box of potential contagions of common colds or flu, Eva stood and followed without hesitation. They skipped past the entrance to the emergency room and toward the elevators around the hall that looped the waiting room. She stopped at a small podium and Denise typed Eva's name into an electronic tablet and it printed out a name tag.

"Here you go."

"Thanks," Eva said.

It didn't take long to reach the floor, Denise guiding her to the room before giving Eva a quick kiss on the cheek and rushing off.

"Knock, knock." Eva stood in the doorway, not wanting to enter without permission.

Mr. Wyman looked up, a few playing cards in his hand. There was a nurse sitting beside him with cards, and more set up on a small moving table.

"You do know, saying knock knock is as unnecessary as you are standing there and staring at us?" Mr. Wyman put another card down, his mood relaxed despite his reasons for being in the hospital. "Uno!" He rushed out.

The nurse frowned. "Yeah, yeah."

A second later, the nurse stood.

"I need to get back to work and you have a visitor."

"I haven't won yet," Mr. Wyman inveighed.

"And you're not going to. Not this round." The nurse smiled and walked past Eva.

"Have fun," she mumbled.

Eva walked into the room, Mr. Wyman grumbling about his displeasure with an unfinished game.

"Shouldn't you be drugged up and barely conscious or something?" she asked. She was surprised to see him making jokes and looking calm after a bad injury. He was in great physical health for his age, but a broken hip and rib weren't easy to recover from.

He moved slowly to put the cards on the table, his first sign of discomfort.

"It's because they have me on such strong drugs that I feel good. I've also never had a decline of energy because of it either. I'm sure when they start to decrease my intake, I'll be a whining bastard," he joked.

Eva shook her head, astonished by how good he looked.

"Well… I'm glad to see that your personality hasn't been affected." She smirked as he looked up to meet her eyes.

His laugh was light, trying not to move as he shook his head.

"Come sit. You obviously knew I'd be well enough to see your latest work."

He pointed at the portfolio that she had forgotten she was holding. She took the seat beside his bed and pulled out her sketches, showing him one at a time.

Mr. Wyman only stared with admiration at her artwork.

"This is Crater Lake, isn't it?"

Eva smiled. "You can tell?" She asked, pleased he'd recognized it.

He nodded; brows stretched high.

"These are lovely." He looked up with the serious, chastising look he always gave her in these moments. "You need to submit your work to the art gallery here and apply to run the art program for the high school. Mrs. Grayson is retiring and needs a replacement."

"Mr. Wyman…"

"God. You and my daughter are so stubborn when it comes to doing what's best for you." He frowned, letting out a heavy sigh.

Eva sat back in the chair and waited for him to speak. She knew which daughter he was referring to as he often pointed out their stubborn similarities.

"I know you think that it's better to live a quiet, hermit life, up in that house of yours, but you deserve to be seen too." He huffed when she didn't respond. "That's all I'll say about it. Anyway. My daughter's in town."

Oh, Eva knew that.

"I saw her." Eva hated how low her voice dropped. He noticed too; brow raised in curiosity but didn't question it.

Eva elaborated. "I ran into her outside earlier."

He nodded and she could see his upper lip twitch.

"My daughter is a lesbian and single, if you wanted to know," he said, maintaining a casual look.

"Okay," she replied as if that information didn't matter. But it did. Not because she was interested but because she simply never considered that Sky would be gay. But it would explain some things from their past, not that they had a personal history, but what she'd observed.

Eva never had a crush on Sky or considered the woman an option. Especially not when they were in high school. Where Eva was bullied and socially awkward, Sky thrived around people and was the center of attention. To put it plainly, Sky was the popular, smart, and gorgeous girl and Eva was the loner nerd.

"She doesn't know me, and I don't know her," Eva decided to point out.

He gave Eva a thoughtful look and nodded.

"Well, that's about to change." He smiled.

Eva did not smile, staring at him suspiciously. When he didn't add anything to that cryptic statement, she let it go and went onto lighter topics.

Twenty minutes had turned into almost an hour when someone stepped into the room.

*

Sky was surprised to find the woman from earlier sitting with her dad. They seemed to be joking about something that happened in town and for a second, Sky felt a pinch of jealousy. She was always in the know when she lived here but now, she was clueless and watching her dad laughing with someone other than her.

"Hey!" she announced herself and they both looked up.

The woman stood as if to leave but her dad reached out to stop her, only to wince from a sharp pain that Sky wanted to vanquish.

Sky rushed to her dad's side, hand on his shoulder to make sure he didn't try to sit up. It took him a minute to catch his breath and fight through the pain that she knew he had been pretending wasn't there.

His shoulders loosened and he let out a dramatic breath.

"That didn't feel too good," he joked.

Sky waved her hand out.

"No more goofing around. I'm serious this time."

"You mean you weren't serious earlier?" he teased and winked toward the woman who Sky did not think she'd see again, especially so soon.

The woman averted her head, smart enough not to induce his need to be funny.

"Dad…?" Sky complained.

"All right. Goodness. You are just as pestering as your mother was."

That made Sky smile.

"Good." She leaned in to kiss his cheek and then acknowledged the woman.

Eva pointed toward the door and reached for the portfolio on the table.

"I'll leave you two alone and go."

"No, you won't," Mr. Wyman said, sternly. "No one is kicking you out, right, Sky?"

Sky smiled awkwardly and shrugged.

"Sure, yeah."

That didn't sound like a confident answer, and it only made Eva want to leave even more.

"It's okay, I need to get home. It was good seeing you. Don't get in more trouble than you already are."

Sky watched Eva head toward the door in awkward silence.

"Oh, alright. Come by tomorrow if you can. I get bored easily, sitting around and doing nothing," Mr. Wyman said.

"I'll be here," Sky said, as if she was all he needed.

15

Mr. Wyman smiled graciously.

"I know, but you can't stay with me twenty-four seven."

Eva said her goodbye and was out the door and down the hall waiting for the elevator to come when Sky ran up. Eva turned, surprised to see her.

When their gazes met, Eva tried not to look away, a habit she had when she wasn't ready to face someone.

"I want to thank you again for earlier. You saved my ass," Sky said, not sure what else to say.

Sky was being sweet, and Eva knew that this woman didn't like feeling helpless, at least that's how she remembered her as kids. Always independent and stubborn.

"It's no problem." Eva turned to see how much longer it would take before the elevator reached her floor. It was taking too long.

"I'm also sorry, because the truth is, I don't know your name and I feel like I should." Sky looked sincere and regretful.

"Eva," she told Sky and mentally cheered when the elevator dinged and opened. She walked in and pressed for the lobby.

"Eva who?" Sky asked, wincing at her own question.

Eva took no offense to Sky not knowing her name. Sky didn't owe her anything and they'd never been friends.

Before the elevator closed, she said, "Eva Flowers."

Chapter Three

Sky walked into her dad's ICU room and sat down with not much to say. The woman had given her name, and she still couldn't remember who this woman was. It was driving her insane and Sky nearly pulled out her phone to look Eva up online when she noticed her dad staring in amusement and realized the obvious.

"Who is she?" Sky asked, sitting up straight.

"Eva Flowers. We met at a bar in town and played a game of pool, two years ago. She also gives me art lessons."

Sky groaned. "That's not what I meant. How would I know her?"

"You *don't*... know her," he answered. He smiled innocently as he toyed with his daughter. When she looked ready to complain, he gave her a serious response. "You two attended the same schools throughout your childhood."

Sky leaned back into the chair and stared up at the ceiling.

"Eva..." she frowned, shaking her head. How could she have been around her their entire childhood and not know the woman?

"Why does it matter?" Her father asked. He seemed to study her, watching for any hidden answers she might beat around.

"I slipped on ice today and she caught me. I'm just feeling shitty for not knowing the person who literally saved my ass." Sky sighed. "Even more now."

"Honey. You two were on two different playing fields growing up. Don't judge yourself too harshly."

What was that supposed to mean? Sky decided not to press him on it.

"So, you two are friends?" she asked.

"That's what I said." Sometimes, he had a snarky mouth but so did Sky, so she ignored it.

"But how?" she asked.

"I told you."

"But she's my age."

His brows furrowed. "She is like a daughter to me. Calm down."

Sky raised both hands in surrender.

"My bad. I forget how easy it is to connect with others out here. No big stigmas out here to worry about."

"You'd like her," he said.

Sky narrowed her eyes. She could always tell when he had a double meaning.

"Dad… I'm only visiting and she's…" She pictured her in the *Game of Thrones* Christmas sweater she wore earlier and didn't know what to say about that.

"She's what?" He seemed defensive for the woman.

"She's… just not my type."

"Oh, I'm sorry… thanks for proving my point on exactly why you don't know the woman who saved your ass," he chastised.

"What?" Sky frowned.

"Because you only stick with what feels comfortable and familiar." Her eyes widened and he added, "Have you ever been friends with someone who didn't like the same things you did or didn't care about luxury?" He looked down at her expensive hat and jacket.

"This is the image I need to have at work," she argued. She shook her head, hand stretched out. "No. We aren't having this debate. You need to heal. The sooner the better."

"Well... if I pray really hard, maybe I'll wake up with new ribs and a hip," he said sarcastically before turning the television on to the First forty-eight.

Sky looked at her dad in disbelief but took the win and said nothing, watching an episode with him like old times.

*

"Is that Sky?" Maxine burst out with joy when Sky reached the register. "Oh my god." She rushed around the counter, and they hugged. "I should have known you were coming. How's your dad?"

"He's better than I pictured in my head driving here."

They separated and Maxine headed back around the counter, grinning widely.

"Sorry... what can I get you? Maybe if you have a second to catch up, I can have someone take over."

"Sure, and I'll have a gingerbread chai latte." Sky had been at the hospital all night until the late evening when they kicked her out. She missed the comfort of coming into town for a seasonal chai blend and walking through town with her friends.

She planned to stay in her childhood home. Her dad had kept the house the same since her mom's passing.

It was morning and she was planning to visit her dad but decided to stop at a coffee shop she'd noticed when she drove into town. Sky hadn't seen Maxine in over a year and had been wanting to catch up. They'd been friends since middle school, and nothing had changed except distance.

Maxine took her order and soon they were sitting at a table near the front door.

"You look good!" Maxine complimented.

Sky carefully sipped her drink, staring out the front window that faced the street.

"Thanks. I was able to get some much-needed rest."

"I hear your dad is cracking jokes like his usual self. I assumed that meant he was okay, considering." Maxine reached across the table and squeezed her hand. "I've been meaning to reach out. Things got busy for me here and time flew."

"What's new?" Sky asked, hating how she allowed distance to be the reason to not know what had changed in her friend's life.

Maxine waved her arms out and twisted in a gesture that was easy to comprehend.

Sky's brows raised, caught off guard.

"This place is yours?"

Grinning wide and proud, Maxine nodded.

"As of three months ago. James was promoted with a huge raise and that allowed for us to buy my dream business."

"Oh my god." Sky stood and gave Maxine a hug, happy for her friend. "You have a good man."

Maxine huffed playfully. "Don't I know it."

"Any plans for kids?" Sky asked.

"Not yet. We both agreed that we wanted to enjoy our new business roles and go on our first international trip next year. After our trip, who knows."

Sky beamed, elated at her friend's accomplishments.

"You two are doing everything right."

"Thanks." Maxine blushed and wiped the corner of her eye, a fight to keep her emotions in check. "That means a lot. I wish you were back home. Especially when the time comes that we start having babies. They'll need an auntie up close when they want to escape."

It was hard hearing that. Sky missed her family and close friends, but she couldn't see her career taking off here.

"I miss you so much."

"I miss you too."

They sat in silence until a question came to mind.

"This is random, but do you know someone named Eva?" Sky had found her high school yearbook but there was no such luck as the mysterious Eva Flowers had not taken her senior year photos.

"Umm," Maxine seemed stuck in thought but there was a furtive look that passed through her averted gaze. "I don't think so."

"Are you sure? She's from here." Sky couldn't believe no one knew the woman.

An older woman sitting at the table behind them answered Sky's question.

"She comes in here once a week and works over there." She pointed at a table tucked in the corner next to a sofa. "She works in tech and rebuilt my website last year. She's also an artist."

"Thanks," they both said.

The woman nodded and went back to reading her book.

"Now that I have a face to go with the name, she comes here at least once a week," Maxine admitted.

"And?" Sky asked impatiently.

Maxine laughed. "We went to high school with her."

How could she be so unaware of another person? Was Sky so self-centered back then not to care? It made her regret how uncaring she was to not be aware of someone who was around her since they were kids.

"What's her story?"

"Uh…" Maxine looked awkward and leaned forward. "She was the foster kid, remember. Always had her nose deep in a comic book and never talked. She wore *hand me down* clothes and unfortunately was bullied by a lot of our classmates."

It suddenly hit Sky and the regret only increased.

"She was outed for being gay a few months before graduation at prom. They humiliated her," Sky whispered.

Maxine nodded. "Yeah, that's her. You even tried…"

"I didn't try hard enough," Sky said, disgusted with herself. She'd never forgiven herself for allowing those boys to humiliate Eva all these years and despite all that, she still managed to forget her name and what she looked like.

Sky covered her face; her ignominy was so great that she wanted to hide away. She'd never even known the girl's name that night. How could she not know her name? The girl back in high school had looked so different from the woman she met now. That night had been dramatic and hard for Sky too, standing in front of her classmates and witnessing another girl being outed. She had feared she'd be next and when no one mentioned her name, the least she could do was help the girl who wasn't so lucky. It was selfish to admit, but she felt guilty for not doing anything to stop them, not that she knew what her classmates were going to do.

"What's wrong?"

"I met her yesterday," Sky admitted. "I slipped on ice, and she caught me. And then she was there again in my dad's room. Seems they became buddies while I've been in the city, clueless as to what my dad's been up to. And the whole time, I didn't know who she was. She probably thinks I'm a terrible person."

Maxine shook her head. "You're not terrible. We aren't the dumb kids we used to be, and we never bullied her. I agree… we didn't do much to help, but it's been years."

"No one just moves on from that in a town like this. Where no one forgets a damn thing you did or experienced. I mean, surface level, maybe, but not completely. But what do I know?"

Maxine nodded. "What are you going to do if you see her again?"

The chances of Sky seeing her again were much higher now that she knew the woman was friends with her dad.

"I don't know." Sky finished her drink and sighed.

She stood after a few minutes and grabbed her purse.

"I should get going. I need to make sure my dad doesn't do anything to hurt himself more."

Maxine stood too and they hugged.

"Dinner this week?"

"Deal." Sky left, hoping for alone time with her dad before she faced the woman again.

Chapter Four

"Is there any chance of me at least convincing you to submit your art to the gallery?" Mr. Wyman looked hopeful in his hospital bed, giving Eva his famous pleading eyes.

Eva snorted; legs crossed as she continued her sketch.

"You don't quit." She looked at his jawline, a light stubble growing in from not being able to shave.

"You know I'm right. This town is missing out and so are you," he continued.

Eva waved at him. "You have to stop moving."

He huffed. "You don't need me to sit still to sketch me and you know it."

Eva narrowed her eyes and smiled when he smiled back. She was nearly done, mostly shading.

"By the way, why do you want me to draw you lying in a hospital bed?"

"Personal reasons," he responded.

She looked back up and he smiled.

Eva shook her head. She was done a few minutes later and held it up.

"I look too healthy," he caviled.

Eva turned the sketch to review it and then turned it back to him.

"This is how you look right now. What did you want me to do, add puffy red eyes with a fragile mangled body?"

"Yes. I'm in the hospital with a broken hip and rib, for goodness' sake." He exhaled. "I guess it'll do."

"I can keep it, you know," she motioned to slide it back into her sketch book.

"No, no! I love it."

Eva placed the sketch on the table and sat back down to see Sky coming in. She had an oblique look in her eyes, shifting her gaze to her father.

"Dad." Sky walked into the room; she seemed to struggle to meet Eva's eyes. "Hello, again." She was clearly trying to be polite.

"I wanted to stop by before work." Eva found herself having to explain her reason for being there.

Sky looked down at the sketch on the table and then back up at Eva with curiosity.

"She sketched this for me. I want you to make copies and mail this to your siblings. Maybe if they got a vivid picture of how hurt I am, they would rush here too." Mr. Wyman looked very serious in his request.

Eva on the other hand, looked surprised and uncomfortable.

"Umm… you didn't say anything about me drawing this for you just to make your kids feel guilty."

It was Sky who spoke.

"My dad is just the comedian." She continued to look at the drawing but didn't pick it up. "I'm not mailing that to them."

"Then I'll do it," Mr. Wyman said.

"How?" Sky argued.

He looked so stubborn.

"I have my ways."

Sky rolled her eyes.

The doctor walked in.

"Mr. Wyman. The nurses tell me you've been doing well. I thought it would be the perfect time to do a reassessment."

"Damn... they ratted me out," Mr. Wyman complained.

"They're doing their jobs," Sky corrected.

"It'll only take 15 minutes. You both can wait in the waiting room," the doctor said; a nurse stepped into the room to assist.

Eva and Sky walked out together into the waiting room just outside of the ICU. There were only two benches, one on each side of the small hallway.

Eva waited for Sky to sit so that she could take the bench opposite. She turned for the other bench but hesitated, feeling a strain that left her wanting to leave. She couldn't sit across from Sky in bleak silence and pretend she was comfortable.

"I'm going to head out. Could you tell your father I had to go?"

Eva was about to walk off but found herself turning back to Sky, who was watching her and giving no response. Their eyes locked until Eva turned away.

"Do you have to leave? Because if you are making that up so you won't have to sit out here with me, you can say that." Sky had enough restraint to sound unbothered that the woman clearly couldn't stand being in the same room as her for too long.

Instead of lying or trying to come up with some other explanation that would still be a lie, Eva studied Sky before answering. She looked toward the ICU door and pictured what Mr. Wyman would say to her running away every time she was placed in an uncomfortable position.

Eva sighed. "I'm not really… umm… someone who likes…" Eva hadn't thought about what to say before opening her mouth. She sighed again.

"Is it social anxiety or do you choose to keep to yourself?" Sky pointed toward the door. "Except for the few that sneak through your barrier, like my dad."

Eva's heart continued to pound; Sky's blunt questions were not easy to answer.

"You know, I have to admit it's a little bit of both. I used to want to be social and then as the years added up, fear of being social crept in." Eva was surprised with herself for being honest.

"I know I haven't made it easy for you… being around me. I'm sorry about that. I'm just…" Sky paused, trying to avoid sounding too critical.

"Protective of your dad and want him to get better." Eva shrugged and nodded. "I get that. I certainly don't want to see him experience any setbacks because he thinks he's invincible."

Sky smiled. "Exactly. I've never seen him hurt before. Not physically at least. Always the strong one who can do it all. Other than when my mom passed, he never cried in front of me."

Eva could see that. Though she'd known him for two years, he'd never been sick around her or displayed any physical limitations.

"I'm sure your being here has given him a little extra power though," she joked.

Sky stared up at her for only a second with a thoughtful and inquisitive look before laughing.

"Don't tell him that or he might just try to fly out of here."

Eva smiled back. "I won't."

"Please sit. You don't have to leave," Sky said, not giving Eva much room to argue.

She looked down at the seat and gave in. Eva could admit that it was nice talking to her and not as scary as she thought it would be.

"I'm sorry."

Eva looked up; her elbows rested over her knees.

"For what?"

Sky hesitated and then sighed.

"I told myself I wouldn't bring this up but here I am. I couldn't let go of not knowing who you were. I mean… this isn't a metropolitan city. I should know who you are if you've been here our entire lives."

The nerves Eva had felt earlier skyrocketed back up to the front roll. She'd rather pretend they didn't have a past and start from scratch.

"It's unnecessary. We don't have to discuss anything."

"I just… wanted to say sorry for my part in the past. I'll leave it at that, if that's all you will allow me to say," Sky rushed out. "I'm sorry. I felt like I owed you that much."

Eva frowned, confused by Sky's need to apologize for anything.

"What are you talking about?"

Sky looked perplexed.

"Umm… for not helping you. For contributing by not speaking up about it sooner. The bullying."

Eva sucked in the longest breath before she spoke.

"I've never blamed you or thought you did anything wrong. I never expected you to get into a screaming match or fight with them on my behalf. You told the teachers, and they knew. You did your best at that time. And that night..." Eva looked away, remembering the night a group of classmates broadcasted her sexuality in the most disgusting and petrifying way. "That night, you helped more than you know."

Eva remembered storming away, minutes from removing herself from this earth. It was Sky who talked her down without knowing it. Of course, Eva would never tell her that.

Sky was dumbfounded, unprepared for how to respond. She'd assumed Eva didn't want to be around her because of their time as teens.

"Then why do you keep trying to bail every time I'm around?" she asked.

"Wow..." Eva shook her head. "You have not changed when it comes to wanting to know something." Sky frowned and Eva explained. "I remembered anytime a teacher said something that made no sense to you, you'd hound them until they gave an answer that you were satisfied with."

"Hound?" Sky questioned with a silly look. "Is that really the word you want to use to describe my inquisitions?"

Eva crossed her arms. "How would you describe it?"

"I was being persistent," she replied.

They both laughed. After several seconds, they gradually quieted and Sky's brow perked up.

Eva snorted. "I…" she sighed. "Fine. It's because of our past that I get uncomfortable around you, and it has nothing to do with what you did or didn't do and more to do with just being reminded of the past by the look in people's eyes when I pass by them. And that's with anyone from high school."

"But you go to Maxine's coffee shop, and she was in school with us." Sky spoke too quickly, giving away just how far she had gone to find out who she was. "I'm sorry. I wasn't trying to invade your privacy or anything."

Eva only waved, not letting her get too stuck in the sorry lane. She'd already admitted she had been trying to find out who she was.

"It's all good. And I go there because she sells good chai tea, and she never bothers me. She has enough customers for that."

"I'm a chai tea lover too," Sky admitted. "Look… you and my dad are friends, so I take it you will be around a lot. Could we at least try and coincide?"

Sky was right. Eva nodded.

"Good." Sky seemed to relax.

A nurse opened the double doors and waved for them to return. They walked into Mr. Wyman's room in silence, the tension from earlier gone.

Eva looked at Mr. Wyman to see him smiling. She knew he was surprised to see her still here and honestly, Eva was surprised with herself. Eva sat in the chair closer to the window as Sky took the chair beside her father's bed.

"What did the doctor say?" Sky asked with no delay.

Mr. Wyman looked from his daughter to Eva, a small smile lifting the corner of his lip.

"That if I continue to be a good boy, I'll be able to walk with the same swag I had before my injuries."

Sky crossed her arms, eyes narrowed on her father. "Anything else?" she grumbled.

"I'll need to do some rehabilitation and be patient with the process." He narrowed his eyes right back at his daughter. "But… I think that last part was meant for you."

Sky didn't skip a beat. "Or maybe he was saying, don't try climbing any ladders before you're ready to walk, since you don't know what taking a break is."

Eva watched with fascination at how alike the two of them were, going back and forth in quick, witty responses. Mr. Wyman had much more of a playful side to his wit, whereas Sky was serious, charming, and witty without trying to be. Eva didn't have personal experience with healthy families growing up. She'd spent most of her adolescence in the foster care system and left the same way she'd gone in; alone.

It was refreshing to see the love they had for each other, and Eva could admit she wanted that for herself. Not just a partner but a whole family.

By the time Eva was done dwelling in her thoughts, both were watching her as if they were about to give her an inquisition.

"Yeah?" she asked. Their equally intense gazes made her nervous.

Sky pointed to the picture Eva had sketched.

"I love this picture you drew of my dad."

"Oh." Eva looked at the drawing on the table. "Well… yeah… it was nothing." She didn't do well with compliments.

Mr. Wyman snorted, shook his head, but said nothing.

"This is not nothing," Sky said. "The way you bring my father to life through paper... it's... naturalistic and enchanting."

Eva stared at Sky, transfixed by the words she used to describe her art and couldn't hold back a smile.

"Thank you." This time, she didn't sound awkward.

"I'll have you know my daughter here is an artist too," Mr. Wyman said proudly.

Sky shook her head, not having the same amount of confidence her dad had in her.

"Not like this. Plus, I haven't done real art of any kind in a long time."

"You're an artist?" Eva was intrigued.

"Right now, I work as a makeup artist, but my passion is being a cosmetic costume artist and stylist. But when I draw, it's more to create a look I want to give to someone."

"That's freaking cool," Eva said, not expecting to share a common interest with Sky of all people.

"Thanks. Like I said though, it's been a minute since I did any art." Sky wasn't someone who normally shied away from a compliment, except when it came to her artistry.

Eva reached for her phone when it buzzed and checked the text.

"It seems work calls for me early. I should get going."

"Thanks for taking time out of your morning to see me." Mr. Wyman smiled and waved his goodbye.

Sky's smile reached her eyes for the first time as she waved her own goodbye. Eva felt a peaceful comfortability settle over her as she left knowing she had fewer walls up today than she ever had before.

Chapter Five

A nurse came in soon after Eva left to help her dad readjust without risking his recovery and Sky took that opportunity to check her texts. She had two, one from her sister Jackie and another from her friend back in the city who'd taken all her gigs for the next two weeks. Sky gave them both an update and looked up to find her dad watching her.

Sky could tell when her dad wanted her to do something that was usually out of her comfort zone. She stared dubiously.

"What?" Sky put her phone away and waited for his requests to start pouring out.

"Have you considered, at least once, moving back?" her dad asked. If it weren't for the broken hip and rib, Sky probably would have tried to shake him until he learned to stop asking.

So instead, Sky sighed and rolled her eyes.

"How many times do we have to go over this?"

He didn't answer. "You should let Eva do a portrait of you."

Sky narrowed her eyes. That was a random change of subject. What was her father up to?

"Why?" she asked.

"Because I don't think you've seen yourself in a very long time. A portrait of you would be a very intimate thing and one that could help you figure out what you need to do next."

Sky wanted to question her dad's motives behind his suggestion and argue against it but as an artist herself, she understood how a self-portrait could make someone self-reflect. It was almost like a visual diary. It could show insecurities and self-deprecating thoughts with the way the eyes in the sketch were highlighted.

Maybe seeing herself in a different texture could help her figure out some things. So instead of arguing against her dad's suggestion, she nodded.

"I'll think about it."

His brows raised, surprised but quickly recovered with a smile. She fought him most of the time, and on rare occasions she accepted that her father could be right.

"What are your plans while you're in town?" he asked.

Sky frowned, unclear of what he was asking.

"Taking care of you, of course."

"Yes, to some degree. But I'll be in a rehabilitation facility for some time before I can come home, and I do plan on hiring a home aid. You need to make sure you stay busy." His eyes widened as he thought of an idea. "The high school is throwing their annual school play and I'm sure the theatre instructor would love if you helped with the designs and doing the kids' makeup."

"Dad?"

"Please don't argue with me on this. I don't want to be the only thing you focus on while you're at home. And you just told Eva you haven't done any art in a while. Here's your chance."

Sky sighed. Again, her dad was right, and she hated admitting that to him because he would not let her forget it. She groaned and waved her arms out in surrender.

"Fine. I'll reach out to the theater instructor and see what they say."

"See... was that so hard?" Her dad couldn't keep that comment to himself.

Sky didn't answer.

"All right. I need a nap and I don't want you staring at me while I try to sleep." Her dad had a unique way of kicking her out when he wanted to be left alone. "Perfect time to go up to the school."

"Now?" she asked.

"Christmas break is right around the corner," her father pointed out. "No sense in delaying."

Sky stood, seeing no point in arguing.

"Fine. If it will get you off my back, I'll go now."

"Thank you." He pointed to the window. "And could you close the curtains some? You know I can't sleep with the sun in my face."

Sky laughed, shut the curtains, and kissed her dad. She left before he said anything else.

*

The high school had doubled in size since she graduated over a decade ago; the main entrance was no longer in the small building she used to walk through as a teen. They'd built a new building two stories tall beside the old one and painted it pale blue to resemble the partial school colors.

Sky walked inside, a receptionist greeting her as she approached the desk and asked to meet up with the school theater instructor. If this were a large city, the chances of Sky being seen without an appointment were slim, but here, walk-ins were welcome.

"He will be with you in a moment," the receptionist said. "Here's a name tag. Please sign in and then you can have a seat over there." She pointed to the seats behind Sky and smiled.

Sky checked in and took a seat just as she noticed a man with dark hair and a light tan complexion come down the hall. Sky recognized him right away.

"Chas!" She leaped to her feet, and he smiled widely, rushing down the hall. They embraced. "Oh my god," she said, shocked to see him. "I thought you were still in Spain. When did you get back?"

Chas spun her around as if she weighed nothing. He was brawny and had a gentle touch. He had a clean shaved head with the most beautiful, unmarked dark creamy skin that every girl wanted.

"I've been back for almost a year. I heard you were in town. What are you doing here?" he said excitedly.

"My dad—"

He put her down and hunched exaggeratedly.

"We all know about your dad. I mean... what are you doing here..." he waved his arms around. "In this school?"

"Oh," Sky laughed. "I'm here to see the theater teacher."

"Well shoot. Here I am, baby," he said in a sassy voice.

It had been almost seven years since Sky had seen Chas. His last words, *I ain't coming back,* were what pushed her to leave and follow her own dreams. They'd grown up together and he'd been a closeted bisexual until the year before he left to go abroad.

"Come on." He guided her down the hall, through the back entrance where they crossed to another building. Using his fob to open the door, he proceeded to give her a tour of the remodeled building she used to frequent every day for four years. There were classrooms on both sides of the building and his theater room was tucked in the back, across from a large art room.

"Welcome to my humble abode," he said, flaring his arms out as if finishing a performance. "How might I assist you?"

Sky shook her head. "No. Story first. I need to understand how you came to be back here."

He smiled. "Always needing to know," he teased. Chas explained that he'd left out of fear of being judged when he came out and thought drastic change was the way to go. But in the end, he didn't realize how awesome he had it until he left. Life here was always warm and exciting. He came back and hadn't regretted it.

"Seriously, you clearly didn't know I was the theater teacher, so I know you didn't come here for just a chit chat. How may I be of service?"

Sky laughed and explained why she was here. She couldn't even finish before he leaped out of his seat with excitement.

"Do you know how long I've dreamt of us working side by side? The artist of dramatic expressions and sounds. And you…" he looked up at the ceiling as if star gazing. "A true artist of bold visuals and masterful effects."

Despite her initial hesitation, she was glad she'd come.

"You are sure I'll be able to help?" she asked.

"Most definitely. My students have not been assigned roles yet, which will be before holiday break, but the play is a personal piece I wrote. It's *Dracula* with a twist. Trust me... I was in dire need of a costume makeup artist. Plus, this year we are going to be filming it. I have a few students who are trying to join major theatre productions, and two bound for Juilliard when they graduate. This could be the submission piece they need. And who knows. It might bring us other opportunities for the future. I see big things. Even opening a theater production in this beautiful town of ours."

Sky was amazed by the vision Chas had in growing the town but also helping his students reach bigger dreams in the theater world than he was given.

"Will this be the original version of Dracula with the long claws, sharp pointy teeth, and theatrical expressive art or modern-day Dracula?"

Chas pressed his hand over his chest as if offended by the question.

"The original, of course. Dracula is not meant to be charming and sexualized."

Sky rolled her eyes.

"My bad for even asking."

"Already forgiven," he teased. Chas went to his desk and grabbed a DVD from his drawer and handed it to her. "Watch this and you'll get an idea of how the costumes should look."

She read the cover. "Dracula."

"It's the 1931 masterpiece. The difference will be that Reinfield," he paused to explain who the character was, "he is who becomes enslaved to Dracula. Anyway, in this twist, it is Dracula who will end up being enthralled by

Reinfield, finding him to be his salvation. As for Mina and Van Helsing roles, you'll have to wait and see."

"Sounds interesting and inclusive to sexual orientations." Sky admired Chas's creativity and boldness in crafting a play that could be subject to scrutiny. They were living in a town that still had a conservative side.

"Many of my students are LGBT. I was relieved to come back and experience some big changes in how diverse and inclusive our town is." Chas did seem right at home and more comfortable here than he had during their entire childhood.

"The only thing I'm missing is someone techy to help with editing and someone who could draw out each student, like an individual and collective portfolio.

Sky's eyes widened and then narrowed a second later. Was her father so informed of who was running the theater program and what was needed that he had purposely orchestrated this? Maybe, he didn't have Eva draw a picture of him to just send to her siblings. He wanted Sky to see how amazing Eva was as an artist. So, Sky could what? Recommend Eva to Chas as a potential assistant to his theater program? No, her dad couldn't be that calculating, especially while lying in a hospital bed.

Then again, since he had no choice but to be still it also meant he had ample opportunity to strategize. And she'd learned Eva also worked in tech.

Hmm.

Chas studied Sky, wanting to know where she'd drifted to.

"Care to share?"

Sky looked up. She'd be foolish not to mention Eva at all.

"Do you know Eva Flowers?"

He shrugged. "I know of her. I mean, we went to school with her." He sat back down and crossed his legs. "I tried to strike up a conversation with her once, but she didn't bite." His eyes perked up with curiosity. "She does hang out with your dad at Irby's Tavern sometimes. Why do you bring her up?"

"She saved my ass the other day and since then I've been bumping into her at the hospital. She visits my dad."

His brows raised mischievously.

"Bump in, huh? Didn't think she was your type," he joked.

Sky tried not to come across as insulting Eva and shrugged.

"It's not like that. She's literally just been hanging around with my dad." Chas looked too intrigued for Sky's liking, and she continued. "Anyway," she said dramatically. "I heard she works in tech, and I definitely know she is one of the best artists I've seen... ever."

Chas ran the tips of his fingers over his chin.

"Really?" He frowned. "But would she be interested? She doesn't seem like someone who wants to get involved in the social scene and this would put her in the spotlight."

Sky knew he was right, but she knew if anyone should be doing the artwork he needed, it should be Eva. There had to be a way to convince her to join.

"Leave that to me," she said.

"Mmm." He smirked.

"Stop that. She's my dad's friend." And the truth was, Eva wasn't the type of person Sky went for. As far as looks were concerned, Eva was pretty in her own way. But she was also an acquired taste Sky couldn't figure out, nerdy and socially awkward.

Sky wanted someone who could stand beside her, not blend into the background. Someone who loved to be active and experience luxury things from time to time. Someone confident and open to connections. Eva didn't seem like any of those things. That wasn't a bad thing, it just wasn't Sky's thing.

"Let me know how that goes. For now… how about you come back later this week and see all the kids as I assign their roles. You can start planning their looks."

"Sounds great."

"Great," he responded, standing as he looked at his watch. "Lunch is almost over. I'll walk you back to the front. I teach public speaking next."

They walked back up to the front, making small talk, and Sky left feeling pleased with herself and her future. It made sense to do something fun while she stayed to support her dad's recovery.

Sky climbed into her car and wondered where to head next. She didn't know if Eva would be returning to visit her dad again and she didn't know where she worked.

Taking a risk, she texted Maxine to ask if Eva was working in the coffee shop today. To her surprise, Maxine replied quickly, confirming Eva was there in her usual spot. With a new mission in play, Sky decided she'd spend some time at her dad's house and head to see Eva later, to give herself enough time to come up with a speech that would convince her to join the theater program. Besides, it hadn't been long since they departed, and she didn't want to bombard her so soon.

She'd figure out what to say and cross her fingers.

Chapter Six

Eva listened to her client on Zoom. Most of her day consisted of several meetings where she had to do a lot of explaining rather than doing.

"It will take more than a few weeks to add in the featured designs you want and a lot more money than you budgeted for. I promise you… it's not necessary and I want to make sure you're successful in the timeframe that the site is scheduled to be released."

After some much-needed persuasion, Eva shared her screen to show the client the color scheme and typography samples she'd come up with, explaining the vision behind it as she heard the doorbell lightly ding. She looked up from her laptop and saw Sky walk into the coffee shop, unraveling a dark wool scarf from around her neck. Eva was tucked in the back corner, able to watch Sky without being obvious.

It surprised her when Sky directly looked her way as if she'd known where she would be seated. Their eyes locked but Eva's attention was drawn fully back to her clients, so she didn't seem distracted.

There was something about Sky that Eva hadn't wanted to see before. Sky had a statuesque presence that made everyone around her want to look. She wore a long black skirt, black boots, with a crop top and leather jacket. Eva couldn't understand what planet the woman was from. It was 40 degrees outside.

She finished her presentation faster than she expected and after a few changes her client wanted to see, she agreed to send them a few more options and work on a few logo variations. Eva ended her video call and slid her headphones off, quickly adding to her notes on Figma before closing her laptop.

She looked up to find Sky standing in front of her table. Eva's eyes opened wide.

"Uh… hey," she said awkwardly.

Sky smiled. "Are you still working?"

"No," Eva said. "That was my last client for the day."

Sky pointed at the chair on the opposite end of the table.

"May I sit?"

Eva looked around, saw a few pairs of eyes cast their way and nodded slowly, trying not to make a big deal out of it. She always sat alone and had built up a reputation of being a loner other than Mr. Wyman, her ex-roommate, turned close friend, Sabrina, and the ER tech she'd secretly dated briefly, Denise.

Eva tapped her fingertips on top of the laptop, aware of Sky's scrutinizing gaze. She didn't look like someone who should be sitting beside Sky and that added to the awkward feeling in her gut. She tugged her beanie down further, close to her eyebrows and let out a breath.

"Is there something you needed?" She was ready to go home.

Behind Sky, the owner of the coffee shop, Maxine watched from across the room as she wiped one of the empty tables. There was too much attention on them, on Eva, and she didn't like it.

"I'm sorry if I'm imposing on your time. I don't have your number, so I had no way to reach you." Sky narrowed her eyes and followed Eva's line of sight as she looked toward the few people who were watching them. Some turned away when Sky locked eyes with them.

"Would you rather we walk and talk? I promise, there is a reason I came."

Oh, so this wasn't you trying to be friendly, she thought. It bothered Eva that it was because Sky needed something from her. That was the only time anyone tried to talk to her in the past, if they needed something and of course, she'd do it.

"No need," Eva said. "What do you need me to do?" She sounded impassive and Sky knew that she'd triggered something.

Sky waited and paused. Maybe this was a bad idea. The last thing she wanted to do was make Eva feel like she was being used. Would Sky be here sitting beside her if not for what she'd initially come here to ask? Sky knew the answer and that made her feel even more guilty. She stood, aware of the mixed signals she was giving off.

"I'm sorry. Never mind. You have a great day."

And like that, she turned, walked off and spoke to Maxine briefly before she left.

Eva stared, dumbfounded. She couldn't figure the woman out and thought it was best not to try.

Maxine came over, her smile a little too big for Eva's comfort. She seemed to be fighting back words enough for Eva to see that what came out of her mouth was not at all what she really wanted to say.

"You need anything else?"

"Uh, no!" It was time to pack up and leave. She put her sweater on over her neon green Polo and stood.

"Thanks for being a loyal customer," Maxine said randomly. "Your support in my business has been a big help."

Eva believed in supporting small local businesses, especially when they were run by black owners. She'd intentionally left very big tips in the jar every week and joined Maxine's monthly subscription that gave unlimited coffee, still buying other drinks since she usually preferred tea. And until now, Maxine had never spoken to her since opening the shop other than to take her order. Why was she now?

Her thoughts seemed to translate through her expressive face because Maxine answered her unasked question.

"You do know that… uh… you don't exactly give off the energy that you want to be bothered. I know in high school things were a lot different for you and you had every reason to close off. But… I think now, most people just want to finally know who you are. You just don't seem like you want people to."

Every ounce of Eva wanted to snap out an emotional response but that was not like her and deep down, Maxine was right. The question was, would Eva ever open up to the people she'd seen all her life or stay in seclusion? Could she handle the potential disappointment? She'd never risked her heart to the people here, except once and that hadn't ended well. Not since that night her personal life was broadcast.

Eva nodded. "Thank you. See you next week." She walked off and Maxine stared, wondering if her words mattered at all.

Only time would tell.

*

Almost a week passed, and Eva had not left her house since she'd encountered Sky at the coffee shop. She had a lot to consider, and the truth was, she didn't want to face Maxine's words. So, she cocooned or as Mr. Wyman called it, hibernated.

Most of the day was spent editing a video a gamer wanted to stream on his channel. Eva played video games but mostly preferred watching gamers as of late. When she noticed the gamer posted on Discord that he needed a graphic designer, she jumped at the chance since she was a huge fan of his gaming.

She was nearly finished and decided to take a break. It was time for dinner and then she'd probably read well into the night before going to bed.

There was a knock at the door and Eva got up, knowing exactly who it was. She opened it and saw not only Denise but also Sabrina. Her brows lifted, caught off guard to see them both and stepped to the side to let them in.

"You are done living in a hole." Denise walked into the kitchen and dug through a drawer to grab a corkscrew to open the wine she brought.

Sabrina cleared the dining table, putting Eva's laptop and additional keyboard over on the small table in the corner of the room and placed the food at the center of the table. She wore a green skin-tight dress over her wide curvy figure, her hair cut into a short afro fade that gradually shortened at the sides and back. She always looked like she was going out later, but Eva had known

Sabrina long enough to know she'd be going home to her bed.

"You haven't answered any of our texts and that means one thing," Sabrina added, finding plates in the cabinets closest to the fridge.

Eva decided to go sit at the table since that was where they'd all end up.

Sabrina placed three plates on the table, with the pizza and wings she'd brought at the center.

"We hate it when you don't answer our texts," she pointed out.

"If it was an emergency..."

"Yeah, yeah," Denise interjected. "We would have called. That's not the point." She handed Eva a glass, placed another next to where Sabrina was seated, and held hers. "You can't keep doing this."

"Doing what?" Eva asked as if they hadn't been through this before.

"Hide away and hope that people forget you, so that when you come back out, you can act like you're starting over and able to stay hidden in plain sight."

"And magically people will take the hint and leave you alone," Sabrina added.

They both looked to Eva for some kind of confirmation that they were right. Eva sipped on her wine and reached for the pizza.

"You have nothing to say?" Sabrina frowned, crossing one leg over the other.

Eva shrugged and grabbed two slices.

"Like what?"

"I don't know," Denise said sarcastically. "Like... what happened to trigger your need to be in seclusion?"

"Nothing," Eva said, and took a bite. She hadn't planned on ever discussing anything because there was nothing to discuss.

"You know everyone talks, right?" Denise said, clearly dumbfounded that Eva was working so hard to pretend everything was normal.

Eva nodded and ate, eyes on her pizza. She hadn't eaten all day, and a slice of bread with buttery garlic, cheese, and pepperoni was just what she needed.

"Then you shouldn't be surprised that people noticed Sky Wyman sitting with you at the coffee shop." Sabrina studied Eva's reaction and groaned when nothing was said. "Seriously, that's not something you hear every day. And then right after, you go AWOL," she added.

"Who is Sky, anyway?" Denise asked. She'd only moved here four years ago.

"She was only the hottest, most desired girl in school and in this town, really," Sabrina answered.

"Well… I've never had a crush on her, so it's not a big deal," Eva said. And it was true. There was no reason to have a crush on Sky. Back then, Eva was always in survival mode and knew her lane. She never thought she could end up with a girl like Sky, so she never allowed herself to even picture it. Besides, she assumed Sky was straight. Sky was still well loved and adored by most and Eva was not.

"No one's saying that you like her," Sabrina said. "What I'm saying is that you were seen with her, and I can imagine the unwanted attention that gave you."

"I like my privacy," Eva said and knew she sounded defensive.

"So do many," Denise replied. "And because of that, we didn't work out. You didn't want people to talk about us if they saw us together."

Eva looked at Denise and saw the hurt that still lingered in her eyes even after a few years. They'd agreed to be friends and it worked out. She only nodded.

They were quiet and Eva knew it wasn't easy being her friend. She cared too much what others thought, whether she wanted to admit it or not. Eva hated being seen because that meant there was a higher chance of someone judging her. She'd known how bad that made her feel before and didn't want to experience it again.

"Why can't you believe that most people want you to be happy?" Sabrina asked.

Eva doubted that statement, brows pinched into a frown.

"You can't really believe that after all these years, everyone who was a jackass to you back then would still be that way now. I talk to some of these people... and they have grown up so much. Some even ask about you. They're just too afraid to reach out because you give them absolutely no room."

"I like my quiet life. I love this home and the seclusion. I love... no one in my business or questioning my lifestyle." Eva was tired and didn't want to hear how she was the problem.

"So... is that a hint you want me to shut up?" Sabrina said.

Eva grimaced. She'd worked so hard over the years to be comfortable with being alone and it was a fortunate surprise when she was given a chance to know Denise and Sabrina. There was no regret in that.

"No, of course not."

Denise only ate and watched; fully aware Sabrina had all the shiny words to say.

"I do not doubt that you love your time away from the world. It's peaceful here. But I call bullshit on you being happy, as an outsider to this town and its people. If you really wanted seclusion, you would have bought a house much further away and never come into town." Sabrina reached across the table, placed her hand over Eva's, and smiled. "No one is saying to forget what you've been through. Only that there is a way to heal from it and give others the opportunity to see what they could have had all along."

"You deserve happiness," Denise whispered. "You deserve to be in love and have the family you want. You are so special and it's selfish not to show that off."

Eva sighed. She appreciated that they cared and never gave up on her.

"I'm sorry. I know I don't make things easy." Eva looked at Denise and sighed. "And I'm sorry, especially to you. My issues placed you in an uncomfortable position. You deserve to be seen and wanted and for someone to do that loudly and proud. I've been kept in the shadows and that didn't feel good."

"Thank you." Denise shed a tear and wiped it away before it slid further down her cheek. She drank the rest of her wine and sighed. "Can we all at least agree that Sky is gorgeous?" she joked.

Everyone laughed and Eva stared at both her friends, relieved to have them in her life. Maybe they were right, and it was long overdue to open up. Eva wasn't the same fragile girl she used to be, and she needed to trust that. If her worst fears came true, at least now she was stronger and had amazing friends to catch her.

The only question now was how she'd put herself out there more. She couldn't just go walking up to people and introducing herself as if they didn't know who she was. And that would be so awkward. Eva guessed the biggest thing she could take from her friend's intervention was that she would at least begin to try.

Chapter Seven

Sky held her breath as she watched the doctor reassess her dad for the final time. He was heading to a rehabilitation facility, with the ambulance waiting outside to take him away. The doctor looked at her father when he was done and smiled.

"You are doing so well, and I have all the faith that you'll recover with no limitations." The doctors' words were like gold to Sky's ear. He looked at Sky and added, "I'll let you two have a moment, give the EMTs the paperwork and he'll be off to charm some new people."

"Are you admitting that I've charmed you, doctor?" Sky's dad asked.

The doctor laughed and nodded.

"You will be missed, Mr. Wyman. And please get better because my dad has missed you there for poker night."

The doctor left and Sky let out breath.

"This is good news."

"I told you it would be," he said calmly. "I'm going to be fine. And a surprise visit from your sister helped."

"I told you Jackie was coming," Sky said.

He nodded. "You did."

Sky looked toward the door and then away in frustration.

Her dad smiled. "She's fine."

Sky snorted. "I'm not worried. I just figured she'd want to be here for you since y'all are buddies and all."

The look in her dad's eyes was filled with humor.

"She's called me every day and if something really happened, she'd know. One of her friends works here."

"But still," Sky said. She couldn't let it go.

"Honey. Eva tends to hibernate. Mostly when something happens." His brows lifted in suspicion. "Did something happen?"

"Like what?" Sky frowned. "Last I saw her was at the coffee shop when I tried to talk to her. I mean… I felt her walls go up and backed away but that was it."

"Oh." He smiled as if that explained it all.

"What?"

"An unexpected visit and in the open. That could do it," he said.

"Do what?"

"Bring attention her way," he said, as if it was obvious. "Honey, you must understand… Eva doesn't do social gatherings. She might go to a bar, but she sits in a corner alone. She might go to the coffee shop, but alone. I think she gives me a free pass because honestly, I'm an old man so I don't count. But even the few friends she has… they only hang with her at her house or theirs or something outdoorsy, probably. Very rarely she'll go out in public. And you just walked over and sat down."

"I asked first," Sky said, shocked it was her sitting down at the table that pushed Eva into hiding.

"She's too polite to say no," her dad said.

Sky frowned. "Is her social anxiety that bad?"

54

Her dad only looked at her with chastising eyes.

"You don't know her."

There was a knock at the door which ended the conversation. What did her father mean by that? Sky needed to slow down and not allow her annoyance at Eva disappearing on her dad have her say something poorly during her next encounter with the woman. Her dad was right. Sky didn't know Eva, and she needed to give her some grace.

Sky stepped to the side and watched as the EMTs carefully maneuvered her dad onto the gurney. He didn't cry out in pain like she imagined, and she was relieved to see him smile.

"Once you're settled, I'll come by to visit and bring you some things to feel more comfortable there." She kissed her dad on the cheek and watched them wheel him away.

There was still a huge chunk of time in the day, and even though she had dinner plans with Maxine, James, and Chas, Sky still wanted to head over to the coffee shop and talk.

It took ten minutes to get there. She parked and walked in, not expecting to see Eva in her corner. But still, when she noticed the area was empty, Sky found herself disappointed.

Maxine waved and after a few minutes, they walked over to a table and sat.

"Are you here to tell me you've decided to leave and give me a goodbye?"

For some reason, it bothered Sky that her friends were counting down the days until she left to return to the big city.

"No. We're still on for today. I just wanted to see you. My dad's probably at the facility by now and I was feeling a little lonely."

"Oh, well you are always welcome to come and work," Maxine joked.

Sky laughed. "I'm sure, soon as holiday break is over, Chas will have my schedule filled. But... if you ever need help in the mornings, I'll be your girl." Sky casually looked over to where she last saw Eva and sighed.

"You really like her, don't you?" Maxine said.

"What? No!" Sky realized how that sounded and squeezed her eyes shut and let out a breath. "I was just talking to my dad how she hasn't come to visit him, and he pretty much told me that her disappearing is normal."

"And he's right." Maxine gave Sky a thoughtful look. "You can like her as a person, you know. It's okay to admit she was growing on you, no matter how brief your interactions were."

Sky nodded. "I know. And I didn't mean for it to come out that way."

"And... it would be okay if you liked her as more than a friend too," Maxine smiled widely. She held her hand up before Sky said something. "I'm not saying that you do like her. All I'm saying is that... despite however she tries to hide herself, she's funny, passionate, has a career, and ..." Maxine hesitated, lips pursed as if she had a secret to tell.

Sky brows rose. "And... what?"

Maxine smirked. "All I'm saying... is she acts like she has no game... but she does. She just doesn't show it. She might not look like your typical polished lovers of the past, but she is sexy in that nerdy stud way."

Sky crossed her arms. "You sound like you know her a lot more than you say."

"Uh…" Maxine smiled, awkwardly. "Six years ago, before I met my husband, I returned here miserable from my failed attempt at a big city life."

When Sky initially moved away seven years ago, Maxine had joined her only to return after a year away. Sky had no idea what Maxine was about to reveal.

"I was depressed, sitting on a bench at a park and she walked up and said something really sweet to cheer me up."

"Really?" Sky said, surprised.

"She's very caring that way." Maxine sighed. "One thing led to another and after a few encounters, she invited me to her place for dinner and we slept together. We were beginning to build something real until I unfortunately screwed things up by asking her to keep our relationship between us."

Sky closed her eyes and sighed.

"That sucks. But I know you didn't mean to hurt her."

"It wasn't about being embarrassed to be around her or anything. I just didn't want to give my parents anything else to be concerned about at the time. And telling them I was bisexual would have been big."

"I get that."

"I missed out but… I met my husband and I'm happy. We have a healthy non-monogamous lifestyle that we tend to keep private in this town, but we live the way we want. All I'm saying is… during that time… I got to see a side of her no one had, and it was… beautiful."

"Why did you pretend you didn't know who she was when I asked about her?"

"Honestly, I freaked out. It's not every day someone asks about her. She also asked me a few years ago to keep our past in the past. She saw you visit a couple years back and thought I was going to tell you."

"I don't remember seeing her." Sky couldn't picture a moment where they had crossed paths.

"You didn't. I'm only telling you this because... I still care about her. I don't want you missing out on getting to know her, if she stops running long enough."

Sky appreciated her friend's honesty.

"I won't mention anything," she promised.

Maxine looked up when the door opened and smiled. "Here's your chance." Maxine stood and winked at Sky before she moved to the side.

"Your usual?" Maxine asked the customer who walked in.

Sky's back was turned, but it was obvious who it was. She had to look up anyway to confirm and found herself contemplating whether she should give Eva the opportunity to speak before she said something.

They'd barely reached a surface level connection the one time they talked at the hospital, and it had been one of Sky's favorite conversations to replay in her mind. It had been honest, sweet, exposing, and fun. The conversation was fluid and transactional, with both of them heavily invested in the couple minutes shared. Sky hadn't experienced a connection like that in a long time and part of her could admit it was more than Eva not showing up for Sky's dad. It was not showing up for her too. Without stating it, they'd been a two-person team, keeping her dad company when the other was away. She could see the potential of them building a friendship that she hadn't considered before.

Eva's hands were hidden in her pockets as she answered.

"Yes. One to go, if you don't mind," she told Maxine who nodded and headed back to work.

Since Sky was seated at the table closest to the register, she didn't want to assume Eva stood close to talk, but when she looked up and noticed Eva's tentative gaze, she could only wonder.

"I heard your dad was moved to the facility here in town." Eva rocked on the balls of her feet, nervous to make small talk.

Sky nodded. "Yes, he was. An hour ago. I'm sure he'd love to have you visit." Sky twirled her cup around and waited for Eva to speak again.

"He knows I'll be there when I can," she said.

"Does he?" Sky's tone was a little too abrupt and she took a breath.

Eva only stared. Maxine waved for her to come get her drink and she pulled out cash to pay. Sky watched the encounter as Maxine declined the money and Eva instead placed it into the tip jar. Sky would have never noticed the awkward and yet unvoiced past between Maxine and Eva, if not for knowing their history.

Drink in hand, Eva turned to say bye and looked surprised when Sky stood.

"Yeah?" She looked nervous, eyes darting around to see who was watching.

Sky sighed. "Where are you going?"

Eva stared, dubiously. "Umm, on a hike."

"Oh." Sky grimaced. When was the last time she went hiking? Years ago, that's when. She needed to try and get Eva to drop her guard long enough to see if they could possibly move past the awkward hot and cold tension. "Could I join you?"

"On a hike?" Eva stared as if she expected Sky to recant.

Sky laughed. "Yes. I hike." She noticed Maxine narrow her eyes, well aware that Sky did not hike.

Eva looked Sky over and assessed what she was wearing.

"You don't look ready for a hike."

"Okay…" Sky agreed. "But I have sneakers in my car and a sweater."

"Uh… it's not an easy hike," Eva admitted.

Did the woman really not want her to go or was she being serious? What did a hard or moderate hike look like?

"Don't I look in shape to you?" Sky said, arms stretched out.

Eva sighed. "Okay, if you're sure."

"I am."

Eva nodded.

"Let me get a couple egg bites for snacks and I'll meet you outside," Sky said.

Again, Eva only nodded.

When she was gone, Sky rushed to the register and looked desperately at her friend.

"What did I just do?"

"You found a way to enter her world and get to know her." Maxine smiled and handed her a bottle of water and fresh egg bites. "Good luck."

Sky groaned and left the coffee shop, not sure if she'd survive the hike.

Chapter Eight

They were thirty minutes into the hike and Eva had to admit she was shocked to see Sky had lasted this long. The hike in total was almost four miles with an elevation of three-hundred feet and by the way Sky panted with every step, she knew the woman was no avid hiker like she claimed.

Eva had originally planned to do the longer hike until Sky asked to join and thought it was best not to torture her. It was clear Sky wanted to talk but she was too out of breath to say what had been gnawing in her head.

To make things easier, Eva took multiple water breaks to help Sky catch her breath. Eva would casually sip from her Hydro Flask backpack and sneak a peek at Sky gulping down her water from a bottle. Then they continued, no words spoken and hiked until Eva thought Sky needed another break.

When they reached the halfway point, Eva pointed toward the lake that was well hidden through dense trees. They hiked slightly off trail until they reached several large boulders residing in the water. Eva began removing her shoes and socks, walking into the cold water that reached up to her lower calf before she stepped onto the boulder and found a comfortable place to sit.

She turned to find Sky standing with a look of defiance in her eyes.

It was clear today; the water was not too cold. The sun touched Eva's skin like a warm blanket, and she closed her eyes, letting Sky make the decision to come closer or not.

Eva heard mumbling but soon Sky had crossed the water and was sitting beside her.

"I guess it's obvious that I don't hike," Sky admitted.

"I was going to do a seven-mile hike before you said you wanted to tag along."

Sky's eyes widened before she realized what Eva had insinuated.

"You could tell I wasn't a hiker?" Sky asked, surprised Eva still let her join.

"Your dad mentioned once that he had to bribe you to participate in family hikes. But you seemed eager to join and I didn't want to say no." Eva opened her protein bar and took a bite.

"To be honest, I wanted to talk to you, and I figured this would be the only way." Sky found it hard to admit that.

"I assumed as much. But I do appreciate you going out of your comfort zone to talk to me. I don't think anyone's ever worked that hard to get my attention." Eva took another bite and grabbed a Gatorade, handing Sky one.

Sky took it, grateful since she had nearly drunk all her water.

"Thanks." She drank some and tucked it between her legs before she spoke again, staring down at her hands.

"I'm sorry for bothering you without warning last week."

Eva shrugged. "You didn't know how I'd react, and you don't know what makes me uncomfortable. You didn't do anything wrong."

Sky nodded. "I assumed, based on our one conversation at the hospital, I could just approach you like we were..." Sky paused, hesitant to say what she wanted. "Like we were becoming friends," she finished.

There was a look on Eva's face Sky couldn't read.

Eva considered what to say, lips pursed as she looked toward the water. She tugged her beanie low and sighed.

"I liked our conversation at the hospital," she admitted. "Your dad talks about you a lot and I think I felt safer knowing your name from a distance. I've tried... opening the door to others from the past and it bit me."

Sky assumed she was referring to Eva's history with Maxine. She kept silent.

Eva looked up at Sky and said, "I don't want to get bitten again."

"There's always going to be a risk when you are trying to get to know someone. I can say it felt weird not seeing you at the hospital the last few days. In such a short time, we had a routine going and I liked it. I liked not being the only one there for my dad. It hurt... not seeing you but here I am, risking another bite."

Sky had a good point. Eva had locked herself away without considering who she'd be letting down.

"You're right."

The shock on Sky's face did not go unnoticed.

"Sorry..." Sky giggled, and it made Eva smile. "I didn't think this conversation would go so easy."

"What did you expect?" Eva asked.

"Definitely resistance," Sky admitted.

Eva nodded. "My friends pretty much came over and lectured me on being the culprit to my own loneliness." She looked up. Transparency was the only way to move forward. "And Maxine said similar words the night I saw you at the coffee shop."

"She didn't tell me that," Sky said.

"I don't want to hate—No!" Eva frowned and shook her head. "That's not what I want to say." She took a breath and spoke from her heart. "I don't want to make others feel uncared for by me. I've been trying to protect myself and not considering how this town might feel about one of their own not being open to them. The truth is... I'd do whatever I could for the people of this town, but they'd never know that. So, I figure, if I could learn to open up to you... maybe I could for others. At least just enough for them to know I care about them and this town."

Sky smiled. "I should really start hiding away when I need to do some self-evaluating," she joked.

"My house does bring me the quiet and peace I need."

"I'd have to see this calming house of yours," Sky said, half-jokingly.

Eva smiled.

Sky took the opportunity to look around, the peace and quiet calming her nerves. She wanted to find a way of connecting with Eva without being too pushy.

It was obvious that Sky had more to say, and Eva appreciated the silence that fell between them. The sound of water flowing relaxed Eva enough to lean back on her elbows and close her eyes. The sun kissed her face, and she bathed in it, almost forgetting she was alone until she heard Sky eating something.

She opened her eyes and smiled, watching Sky admiring the scenery.

Sky let out a quiet breath and smiled once she noticed Eva watching her.

"It's beautiful out here."

Eva averted her head and looked toward the trees in front of them.

"My dad would take me here every weekend. He said this was where he proposed to my mom." She felt awkward mentioning her parents and sat up. It felt easy and natural sharing, but it wasn't something Eva was accustomed to doing.

"That's a lovely sentiment to carry on," was all Sky said.

Eva laughed to herself.

"Maybe one day, I'll be able to have more people in my life to share this place with. Not many know how to find this hidden path."

"That's a wonderful thought to have and it means a lot, you sharing this place with me." She smiled and arched a brow. "Since you've opened the door to creating more connections and us becoming friends…" Sky's animated tone was all the warning Eva needed to know a request was coming. "I've decided to stick around for a while and my dad gave me the great idea to help the high school theatre program, and fortunately Chas is the theater school director. My focus would be on making the kids' characters pop out. He also needs someone to fill in the students' personal sides with portraits and sketches of scenes. And someone to edit what's filmed from beginning to end. You're the first person I thought of." Sky smiled, mentally crossing her fingers that Eva wouldn't say no too quickly. "Actually, you're the only person I thought of," she added.

"Uh…"

"I know it's a big request and I'm not asking just because you're an amazing artist. I understand that your memories back at high school weren't like my own. There's pain there. You might say no, but I'd really like to work with you."

"This is a hard ask."

"Then how about you join us tonight and if we can't convince you, then I won't ask again." Sky instinctively offered something she wasn't sure Eva would take. "It would be me, Chas, Maxine, and her husband." By the time she finished explaining who'd be there tonight, she realized how naïve she'd been.

What if Eva wasn't over Maxine and couldn't handle being around them? Sky bit her inner lip and waited for Eva's walls to go up. But as time passed, Sky was no closer to getting an answer.

Eva sat quietly, Gatorade in her hand, stuck with mixed emotions, not wanting to immediately deny Sky's attempts to pull her out of her comfort zone.

"Go big or go home?" Sky joked and gave the silliest grin, brows arched high and hopeful.

"We should finish." Eva packed her bag and stood, aware that she'd need to give an answer.

The boulder was wide enough for the both of them to stand and Sky shifted to her knees, careful not to lose her balance.

"How do you get up so gracefully? You didn't even use your hands." Sky stood to face Eva, not aware of the slippery edges of the boulder and lost her balance.

For a second time, Eva reached out and curled her arm around Sky's back to prevent her fall. Sky flung her arms around Eva's neck and squealed, thankful for Eva's quick reflexes.

"Oh my god," Sky let out an exhausted breath, forehead pressed against Eva's shoulder. "I swear, I'm not this clumsy." She trembled, aware of how close she had come to potentially getting hurt and, in the worst case, drenched in cold water.

"I should have warned you to be careful getting up," Eva said. She reached for Sky's hand and stepped to the side, while she maintained a firm grasp and climbed off the boulder into the water. "Come on, I got you."

Sky looked down at Eva and believed every word. Sky kept her knees bent, stance rigid as she stepped forward and moved to sit so that she could slide off. Cold water brushed the bottom of her feet as Sky stretched her legs down. Once Sky was down, Eva pulled her close and guided her back to solid ground.

Sky released a nervous laugh.

"Trust me. I'm no damsel." She needed to say that after being rescued twice by Eva.

"That's not a word I'd use to describe you," Eva assured.

They put on their shoes and gathered their belongings. Sky found herself staring as Eva took off her beanie to readjust. She had never seen Eva without a beanie on. She had silky black hair, a few inches long, curly at the top with an undercut. It enhanced her facial structure and highlighted her prominent cheekbones.

"What's wrong?"

Sky blinked rapidly and cleared her throat, startled by Eva's voice. She watched Eva slide her beanie back on and looked off toward the trail.

"Nothing. I'm looking forward to the remainder of the hike."

"I bet you are." Eva looked around and pointed. "Follow me."

"Aye aye," Sky joked. She tried not to think about where her mind had drifted to and followed closely behind.

The rest of the hike was more of the same, stopping occasionally to relieve Sky and by the time they made it back to Eva's car, all Sky wanted to do was lie down.

Sky climbed into the passenger seat and groaned. Eva took off her boots before getting in.

"I need a nap," Sky exhaled and closed her eyes.

Eva smiled and started her car. She put on her seatbelt and grabbed her phone from the glove compartment. Before she took off, Eva turned to Sky and decided in that moment, she'd take a risk.

"I'll come tonight."

Sky straightened and looked at Eva in shock but didn't say anything, only smiled, leaned back into her seat, and shut her eyes.

Chapter Nine

"My body hurts." After the hike, Sky had gone home and napped until it was time to visit her dad. She'd come to the facility and found him already bonding with the staff and other patients. He had his own room, and the television was on with the news giving the latest update.

Sky's dad munched on crackers, eyes on the television, as he casually nodded along with his daughter's whining. He sat immobilized by his own pain, careful not to shift his body. Now that the medication had decreased, he felt everything more. Sometimes even breathing was a chore if he inhaled too deeply.

"That woman is a ninja. I nearly fell, again of course, and she caught me like that," she clarified, snapping her fingers.

"Mhm," her dad agreed, still attentive to the television. "I already told you she was special," he mumbled.

"You didn't use those exact words," Sky said, mindlessly looking through her phone. She slouched into the two-seated sofa, one leg draped across, and wished for a massage.

Her dad didn't respond, and Sky looked up.

"Dad... I'm trying to talk to you."

"Yes, my child. I have been listening," he huffed, muted the television, and looked at his daughter. "You are realizing Eva is awesome, something I already knew, and you're processing that."

Sky narrowed her brows, tilting her head to one side, acknowledging his sarcasm.

"I didn't say all that."

"Did you have fun with her even though the hike itself was torturous?" he asked bluntly.

Sky frowned and answered hesitantly.

"Yes."

"Then that's all that matters. She's good for you and you're good for her. She needs a friend like you. Don't question it." He waited for Sky to comprehend his words and when she nodded, he smiled and turned the volume back on.

And like that, the conversation was over.

*

"You sure she's coming?" Chas asked for the third time. They were all seated at the table; a last-minute decision was made to have dinner at her dad's house.

Sky assumed it would be easier for Eva to come if there wasn't an audience of nosy town gossipers lurking around. She wasn't much of a cook but was fortunate to convince Maxine to come early and cook for them.

"She said she would come, and I believe she meant that." Sky couldn't visualize Eva skipping out even if she wanted to. Sky got her phone number before they separated after the hike and the least Eva would have done was text.

"Be patient," Maxine teased, shoving Chas playfully.

Chas leaned back, a glass of wine in his hand.

"Does it look like I know what that word means?"

"No, but you can at least try to comprehend it," Maxine laughed.

Sky tried not to look at her phone to check the time. Eva was only ten minutes behind. Sky could picture her parked around the corner, trying to build the courage to get out of her car. Sky had asked for a lot today and knew it wouldn't be easy for Eva to participate in a social gathering, especially not with people from high school.

There was a knock at the door and Sky leaped up from the chair and smiled at her friends.

Chas and Maxine snuck glances at each other before watching Sky head to the front door.

The dining room was off to the right of the front entrance and Sky let a heartbeat pass before she opened the door.

"You came," Sky said energetically.

"I said I would." Eva stood at the entrance and waited to be let in.

Sky stepped aside.

"Sorry," she laughed. "Come on in." Once Eva was inside, Sky shut the door, turned, and offered to take her grey plaid coat.

"Thanks." Eva handed it to her, then both stood by the door as Eva waited for further instructions. She wasn't accustomed to going over to stranger's or acquaintance's homes and she didn't want to assume she could walk over to where she saw Maxine, her husband, James, and Chas seated.

Sky looked down at the bottle of wine in her hand and smiled.

"Is that for us?"

Eva held it up awkwardly.

"I was told to never come to a dinner empty-handed."

"Normally, that is customary, but you didn't have to bring anything," Sky said sincerely. "I'm just glad you came." Sky waved to her to follow. "Come on."

They walked up to the table, Sky's friends pretending to talk about holiday plans, but Sky knew by their body language that they weren't.

Chas politely stood to shake Eva's hand.

"Hi. I believe we've crossed paths hundreds of times but it's finally nice to meet you. Properly, I mean."

The tension in Eva's shoulders could be felt and all Sky wanted to do was ease the stress. In such a short time, Sky had grown to feel protective over Eva and wondered how she missed out on being her friend much sooner. It was effortless, talking to Eva when she wasn't running. Sky stood, watchful of Eva's body language and hoped she would push through her discomfort.

Eva shook Chas's hand and one corner of her mouth lifted into a small smile.

"Yeah. I... uh know you tried to talk to me once. Sorry, I wasn't too friendly about it."

"It's very understandable," Chas said genuinely.

James stood next, along with Maxine as he offered his hand. Eva took it and when it was Maxine's turn, Sky noticed the tension between Maxine and Eva, neither of them moving in for a hug or handshake. Sky wondered how long it had been since they had interacted one-on-one.

Chas seemed to notice their apprehension and snuck a peek at Sky but made no comment.

"Glad you could make it," Maxine said.

Eva nodded. "Sky was convincing."

"She has that gift," Maxine joked. With that, she sat down beside her husband, and he reached over to hold her hand.

Sky had no doubt that part of Maxine still cared for Eva, and it was mostly regret in how she had handled things that made their encounter awkward. Sky hoped they could clear the air at some point, and both heal.

"Is that a sneak peek for us?" Chas eyes narrowed on the portfolio Eva kept snuggled close to her side.

Eva nodded. "I thought, while I'm deciding what I wanted to do, you'd want to at least see proof of my artistry. Also, I have a website for my entrepreneur tech space." She handed her portfolio over, this one smaller than the other one Sky had noticed the day they first met.

"May I?" Chas asked.

Eva waved for him to look and took a seat beside Sky, while everyone focused on her drawings.

"Wow…" James said, impressed. "These are… beautiful."

Eva smiled and blushed, looking down at the table.

There were several sketches of people and scenic landscapes well-known around town. Sky recognized the lake where they'd hiked today. There was the boulder, and it was the only thing in color in the drawing as if that were the only place the sun shined.

Sky looked at Eva, amazed by how she saw that day and wanted to know more about the meaning behind the drawing. She was well aware of the audience and wouldn't ask about it now.

Chas looked dreamily at Eva's sketches and let out a breath as if he was trying to blow off an attraction.

"Can you also sketch on the spot, without people posing?" he asked.

"Once I study someone's features, their structures, stance, and so on… yeah, pretty much," Eva acknowledged.

"Care to take on that challenge?" Chas asked.

"No. We aren't going to put her on the spot like that," Sky defended.

Eva pulled out a pencil from her pants pocket.

"It's no problem."

Chas smirked, sticking his tongue out at Sky, and handed Eva back her portfolio.

A fresh piece of paper was pulled out from the portfolio and Eva began sketching. Sky was closest and could make out what looked like scribbled weirdly angled lines that didn't seem significant but immediately was left stunned as something began to form. It was like watching a puzzle at the beginning stage, but unaware of what the finished image would be.

"You don't need to study us or anything?" Chas asked incredulously.

Eva shook her head. "I may not talk to people but anyone I've seen more than a few times is already planted in my head." She continued to explain while drawing. "It's only a matter of angles and objects at this point."

They all carried on with small talk, allowing Eva to finish and after ten minutes, she turned the drawing and showed them what she'd done so far. There wasn't a lot of shading or heavy outlining, but it was enough to prove her point.

She'd sketched all of them, except herself, seated, with wine glasses on the table.

"Could you please finish that because it needs to be framed?" Chas joked.

Eva smiled. "I will."

74

"I told you long ago that you should create murals around town and be in our art gallery." Maxine spoke too quickly and winced when she realized the mistake she'd made. She'd been too swept away by Eva's art to think about what her words might insinuate.

Eva failed to hide her discomfort and Sky knew she had to act fast before she got up and bailed.

"My dad is obsessed with your work. He might submit it to the gallery for you if you don't hurry and do it yourself." Sky lifted her gaze to Maxine, and she gave her a small smile back, relieved when Eva didn't react negatively.

Again, Chas gave Sky an inquisitive look but said nothing.

"It's obvious how amazingly talented you are. How about we eat, and I give you my best pitch? You'd be perfect for the job. Well... it doesn't pay but who doesn't love giving back to the youth?"

James laughed. "You're already pitching."

Sky and Maxine left to grab the food sitting in the oven and came back into the dining room without delay.

Meatloaf, broccoli, and mashed potatoes were served, wine poured; Sky ate, thankful to share her evening with her friends and a potential new one. Part of her couldn't imagine leaving once her dad was better. It was hard leaving Maxine and her dad behind every time she came for a visit but with Chas back and her new potential friendship with Eva, the next round would be even more of a challenge.

Chas kept his promise and gave the best pitch Sky had ever heard. By the time they had finished eating, Chas's eyes were on Eva, hopeful she'd say yes.

Sky reminded Eva that there was no pressure to give an answer now and that earned her a death stare from Chas who Sky labeled, *'the impatient one.'"*

"Where's your restroom?" Eva leaned toward Sky and whispered.

Sky pointed to the bathroom and watched Eva until she disappeared around the hall and then turned to her friends to see them watching her.

She frowned. "What?"

"She doesn't need you playing her protector," Chas whispered.

Sky frowned. "I'm not."

"Uh…" Maxine squinted and gave Sky a skeptical glance. "You kinda are, a little."

"I just don't want you pushing her to say yes. She only came because of me begging her," Sky admitted.

"She's an adult. I have no doubt she would tell me no if she didn't want to," Chas said.

Sky loved Chas but had no confusion as to how pushy he could be when he wanted something. She narrowed her eyes and chose not to argue about it further. Instead, he switched conversations.

"And what's with the awkward moments shared between the two of you?" Chas asked, insensitive to the fact that Maxine's husband was seated beside her.

Maxine groaned. "Drop it," she mumbled.

"I can't ask my friends questions now?" he challenged.

"Yes," Maxine muttered, her tone sharper. "But later."

Chas rolled his eyes. "Fine. You can keep your secrets for now."

Just then, Eva walked up, overhearing Chas's last statement. She glanced at Maxine and then Sky before frowning and looking back at the front door. She wasn't dumb and could tell their conversation involved her. She really hated being the topic of people's conversations.

"I should head out. There are still a few things I have to do for work," Eva said. She didn't move closer, standing like a statue, her body screaming to bolt.

Sky wanted to argue but knew better than to push it. "Okay. I'll walk you out."

Eva didn't look like she wanted to be escorted but Sky wasn't going to let her get away that easily. Eva said goodnight to everyone and followed Sky to the front door. Sky handed her coat to her.

Sky put on a jacket and trailed closely beside Eva to her car and stopped short of her door, arms crossed over her chest.

"I'm sorry if anyone made you feel uncomfortable."

Eva frowned and looked thoughtfully at Sky, trying not to sound too offended.

"You do know… I'm quite capable of taking care of myself?"

It took Sky a second to realize Eva was frustrated with her and she was taken aback.

"I know. I just didn't want Chas to scare you off."

"I can handle Chas's pushy behavior. What I don't like is being coddled and treated like someone who can't handle a little pressure. I never said I couldn't speak for myself; I just tend to get uncomfortable with speaking and prefer not to. There is a difference."

Sky realized that she was right. She felt bad and closed her eyes. Soft warm fingers grazed her own as Eva squeezed her hand gently and Sky felt warm all over. She had to take a breath to focus.

"I know it comes from a place of care and I'm not used to anyone wanting to protect me, so it would be idiotic of me to be mad." Eva's brown eyes were lighter, like a small drop of cream to coffee. She studied Sky for a long moment before asking. "Maxine told you?"

Sky couldn't pretend ignorance and wouldn't insult Eva by lying. She nodded.

Eva sighed.

"I swear, she wasn't trying to break whatever promise she made," Sky argued.

Eva waved her hand, no anger present.

"I'm not mad. It was childish of me to ask her not to tell anyone. Y'all are best friends. You should know everything that goes on in each other's lives."

Sky sighed in relief.

"She'll be happy to hear that."

"I could tell Chas was curious and then when I came back into the dining room, it wasn't hard to figure out what y'all were talking about."

"I'm sorry you had to walk in on that," Sky said regretfully.

"I should start collecting rent on the number of times you say sorry," Eva teased. "We as women tend to feel sorry way too much while men have a skill of not uttering it enough. You don't owe me any sorrys."

Sky smiled. "Yeah, it's a bad habit."

Eva smiled back. "I'll have no problem in helping you break that habit," she joked.

When it was just them, Eva couldn't help but express herself more and let her humor show. She gazed at her surroundings and smiled.

"I'll see you around. And please let Chas know I'll think about it and give him an answer before holiday break is over."

"Okay. Please text me when you get home," Sky said.

Eva nodded and climbed into her car. Sky watched her drive off and headed back to the house to find all eyes on her.

"Admit it." Chas grinned with his arms crossed over his chest. "You have a crush on that nerd."

Sky had no clue where his statement had come from and stared back, dumbfounded.

"And before you go defending her, these days, being a nerd is a compliment. I'm a theater geek and I love it."

Sky sucked her bottom lip in, pleading with her eyes for him to drop the questions.

"You really don't know how to read a room sometimes or you simply don't care how you say things!" Sky argued. "Eva could read between the lines when she came from the bathroom."

Maxine's eyes widened. "She knows that you know?"

Sky nodded. "She's not mad," she promised. "She understands that was an unfair request to ask of you, especially after all this time."

"I knew it!" Chas hollered. "Y'all have history."

"And what if my husband didn't know that and you just outed me?" Maxine twisted in her seat to challenge Chas with a glare.

Chas snorted, waving his finger at Maxine playfully.

"Nope. You'd never keep something like that from your man."

Maxine shrugged. "Bite me."

"I like how you took the heat off you," Chas redirected the conversation back to Sky and she mentally groaned.

"There's nothing to explore." Sky was adamant and preferred not to have her actions dissected and have Chas searching for something that wasn't there.

"Are you serious? I've never seen, heard, or even considered you capable of acting the way you were with her." Chas had a shocked look in his eyes. "You have a crush on her."

"No, I don't. She's not..." Sky didn't want to finish the words. It seemed so crude to say, especially a second time around. And at this point, she didn't know who Eva really was. The woman kept surprising her. "I can admit... that Eva is rare, unique, definitely different from the people I hang around and that intrigues me. Doesn't mean I'm crushing on her."

"Okay!" Chas clearly didn't believe her. He sipped his wine and muttered under his breath, "Then she's the little sister you've always wanted."

Sky snorted. "You are an ass. And she could be older than me."

He laughed.

"Did she seem really okay that you knew? She looked irritated when she walked back in here. I assumed that's why she wanted to leave. She overheard this fool." Maxine flicked her wrist, gesturing at Chas as he stuck his tongue out at her.

"She's fine." Sky knew it was more about them talking about her behind her back rather than the topic itself.

"I keep telling her to just talk to Eva and move past it all." James leaned in and kissed Maxine over the cheek. "Maybe now you'll consider it."

Maxine looked at James and nodded.

Sky was about to push in the chair Eva had been sitting in and realized her portfolio was propped against the back leg. She reached down and picked it up, grazing her fingers over the smooth material, tempted to open it. There were a lot more sketches inside that Eva hadn't shared with them and Sky wanted to respect Eva's privacy. She placed it atop the chair and looked back at her friends who were debating how much snow they'd get this year.

It was aggravating to see how easily she allowed Chas's words to bother her as if they held any merit. Sky thought she was a lot more affectionate and protective over the people she cared about, and for him to assume she liked Eva because of those habits made no sense. Perhaps it was because Sky barely knew Eva and she normally didn't react like that to anyone outside of her close friends and family.

It wasn't important to dwell on and they were supposed to be having a fun night, not digging deep into feelings. Sky reached to refill her glass. She noticed Maxine watching and smiled, drinking half the glass before putting it down.

Nothing needed to be said. Maxine could read every thought that passed through Sky's head and wanted to silently make sure Sky knew she was here if she ever needed to talk. Sky gave a reassured nod and joined the conversation, putting her thoughts away.

Chapter Ten

"Any plans for Christmas?" Mr. Wyman had returned to his room after physical therapy to find Eva sitting in a chair.

The next five days had gone by quickly, finishing with the logo variations she'd needed to send off to her client before the holiday. Eva wasn't into big celebrations of the holiday, but she still preferred to not work during it.

Being in foster care most of her youth, holidays held different meanings based on wherever she had lived at the time. Eva had experienced a vast array of foster parents and every holiday that she spent only made it harder for her to enjoy anything. The conservative and religious foster parents wanted to convert and change her while the liberals overwhelmed her with unrealistic parental love. Some acted as if they could relate to Eva's identity, instead of just being a supporter.

No one asked what she liked or how she would want to spend the holidays, assuming she'd be thankful for whatever they did. It felt more like Eva being forced to fit into their concepts of what Christmas, Easter, and even Valentine's Day should look like. She was the person who was without, and they needed to fix that. They wanted to make Eva see what she had been missing. Most holidays were like performances.

As Eva aged, she promised herself to only spend holidays with the ones who mattered. Her friends had come to her house last year for New Year's, but Eva preferred to be alone through most of the more ceremonial holidays.

She purposely avoided thinking about Christmas and was fortunate to have been sick this past Thanksgiving.

Mr. Wyman cleared his throat and Eva looked up. She uncrossed her legs and sat straighter.

"I'll be at home."

"Doing what?" Mr. Wyman wasn't buying it. He could see her fidgeting and wanted to reach over and console her, but with his injuries, he was incapable. So instead, he spoke, preferring for her to realize who she had now in her life. "I've always wanted another daughter."

Eva stared, perplexed. He looked like he had more to say, so she kept quiet.

"And since I've met you… you've given me that." He smiled and held his hand out.

Eva took it but all she could do was stare.

She admired Mr. Wyman and as a kid she visualized having a dad like him. But she'd learned years ago to let go of that fantasy. She was in her early thirties and hadn't considered ever finding a father figure to lean on until meeting Mr. Wyman.

"Now that I've said that, could you at least stop calling me by my last name because that is only reserved for strangers and casual acquaintances. You have long surpassed that and I'd hope you'd know by now, I'm not going anywhere. At least, not now!" he joked.

He always had to say something silly to make her smile. Eva grinned and nodded. Calling him Mr. Wyman was her way of trying to remind herself that he was nothing more than a casual friend. She was afraid to get too close, but he gave her permission to open up and see him as family.

Eva let out a breath and decided not to neglect the chance at building a deeper connection with him. She saw him as a father figure and was grateful he looked at her like a daughter.

"I care about you a lot. I think you know exactly how much this means to me." She had to turn away, eyes tearing up as her voice cracked.

"I do," he said.

A tear fell. She wiped it away and tucked her head lower, embarrassed to cry in front of him.

"We're a lot alike when it comes to not showing our emotions. I learned from my wife that the people who love us want to be there for us. They want to know we need them. Even then... I hadn't expanded that to my kids and close friends until now. So, when you find someone special... let them see everything." His encouragement was wise and honest, leaving no doubt that he had a lesson of his own behind his words.

"Frank..." Eva smiled when he reacted to her using his first name. He was happy and it pleased her. "Thank you for forcing your way into my life."

"Anytime," he said proudly. "And now that I have taken on the father figure role, officially," he joked. Eva rolled her eyes, sensing a lecture coming. "Which by the way, I hope in the future, you call me dad or something." Eva laughed. "I heard you took my other daughter out on a hike."

Eva narrowed her eyes.

"You are aware that since you now consider me as a daughter, it would be weird for you to imply anything between Sky and me?"

He shook his head. "Not weird in the slightest, but nice try."

She huffed and slouched back in the chair.

"She wanted to talk so I took her hiking."

"And?"

Eva pulled her beanie off and ran her fingers through her curly hair. He enjoyed pulling answers out of her even when she wanted to pretend nothing had occurred.

"She asked me to join her and her friends for dinner to discuss potentially assisting with the theater program."

"And how do you feel about that?" he asked attentively, aware of her hesitation and desire not to talk about it. But he also knew if she wasn't ready to talk, she wouldn't be here. She just liked to whine like Sky, knowing damn well she had a lot to get off her chest and work through.

"How do I feel?" she repeated his question, repositioning in the chair and sighing. "Umm." She waved her hand out before she dramatically slapped it against her thigh. "I hated high school. Half the teachers there, who did nothing for me, are still working there. And... I'd be forced to be around people all the time."

"But...?" he asked, sympathetic to how she felt and hopeful she would see past the fears.

Eva had processed her thoughts and then reanalyzed them several more times, unable to figure out what mattered most. But as she sat here now, she knew why she was still struggling.

"I don't want to let my past control me anymore. I do love this town and at a distance... I see the people and how amazing they seem to be." Eva stared out the window, memories coming back of events and random encounters of people she knew by sight, who lived their lives happily and carefree. "Your daughter made a great argument." So did others she knew. "It hurts others when they try, and I deny them. It's not just about me. If I wanted to be alone, I would."

He nodded. "And that's why I think you and Sky are perfect for each other."

Eva chuckled and waved her hands, trying to stop him from saying more.

"We have nothing in common. She's Sky... and I'm me."

"What is that supposed to mean?" He asked.

"We are not each other's types. I'm a weird, nerdy, homebody who only likes to go outdoors and doesn't know how to talk to people without hiding away for several days after. And she's... everyone else's dream girl, funny, confident, likes really nice things, and doesn't even want to be here." She leaned forward, daring him to question that.

"She doesn't know what she wants," was his response.

She snorted and shrugged. "It doesn't matter. I've always been different and because of that, I'm not for everyone."

"We'll see about that," he questioned.

"See about what?" Sky walked in and Eva immediately straightened. She didn't like discussing Sky behind her back and was nervous about what she might've overheard.

But Sky seemed relaxed and not upset.

Eva looked at Frank, afraid that he might tell Sky what they were discussing but he just smiled and let her lean in for a kiss.

"About her helping with the theater program. I'm trying to tell her it would be the perfect opportunity for people to get to know her and even possibly take over the art program."

Sky smiled. "I heard Mrs. Grayson is retiring at the end of the school year."

Eva moaned. Now she'd be doubled teamed.

"What?" Sky lifted her hands. "I won't need to try to convince you to do it, even though it's an amazing idea. Once they all see your art, they'll keep hounding you themselves."

"So, it's okay to state that other people could hound me until I either give in or hide, but for you, it's being persistent?" Eva asked, remembering their previous conversation.

Sky smiled and nodded. "Exactly."

Eva laughed. "I'm done. I need to go grocery shopping."

"Why? I thought you aren't doing anything for Christmas?" Frank questioned.

Eva had forgotten his initial inquisition about her plans.

"Technically, I never said that."

"Fair... but you didn't say you were either," he replied.

"I normally watch holiday movies and make dinner," Eva admitted.

Sky smiled. "That sounds sweet."

"Perfect," Frank said, as if everything made sense.

"What's perfect?" Eva stared confused.

"Sky was going to stay with me for Christmas..." he said.

"I never said that," Sky argued.

He gave her a knowing stare and Sky huffed and crossed her arms.

"How about you two come visit me Christmas morning, because who wouldn't want to visit their loved one, and then after, y'all spend Christmas together at Eva's place. Heck, I haven't even been there, but I hear it's beautiful."

"Uh, Dad," Sky hesitated and struggled to come up with the right words. "You can't assume that Eva wants me in her house or to spend a special day with her. And then... you'd be all alone."

"No, I won't. I have some of my game night friends coming over to spend a couple hours with me. I'll be fine."

"But still..." Sky shook her head and looked to Eva apologetically. "I'm sorry. You do not have to entertain any of this."

Eva snuck a glance at Frank, who had the remote in his hand and was turning on the television. He knew exactly what he was doing.

Eva smiled and asked, "Do you have plans for Christmas?"

What was Eva doing? Did she consider Sky someone important in her life after such a short time? Their potential friendship was new, but it felt strangely comfortable.

Sky sighed and flung her hand at her dad who was now ignoring them.

"He was my plans!" She looked at Eva and didn't want her to feel obligated to ask her to join. "I guess I can call Maxine—"

"Or you can join me," Eva offered. After the words were out, Eva could feel the tension leave her shoulders. She could do this. "I make really amazing cookies."

"Would I have to cook anything? I could bring something," Sky asked, incredulously.

88

They both looked at Frank when they heard him chuckle. It was no secret that Sky did not know how to cook.

Eva answered. "I do all the cooking."

Sky squinted, still doubting the idea of spending Christmas with Eva. It wasn't a bad idea and she thought Eva would be fun to spend time with, but she didn't want to impose.

"Are you sure?"

Eva studied Sky and knew what her answer would be.

"As long as you want to come, I'm sure."

Sky smiled. "Well… okay then. I'd like to."

They both stood, awkward and unsure what to say next.

Eva took the opportunity to leave.

"I should get going. I like to go shopping when no one's around."

"Oh, and I have your portfolio. You left it at my dad's house," Sky said.

Eva had been meaning to ask for it but was afraid to text Sky, which sounded ridiculous the more she thought about it.

"I can grab it from you on Christmas."

"Great," Sky said.

Eva nodded. "Great." She needed to go. "See you Christmas morning… Frank," she smiled and slid her beanie back on.

He waved with the remote in his hand and smiled as she left.

Chapter Eleven

It was Christmas Eve and Sky had plans to meet Maxine at the bar for a lady's night out. She got there first, the place crowded with groups of friends and couples with similar ideas in mind. To have fun and drink as much spiced apple cider as possible.

Sky ordered two spiced apple ciders, aware of the amount of rum that would be inside. She also grabbed bottled water and found an empty table toward the center of the bar.

Off to the left was a small open space where people mostly danced. The floors squeaked as the bar still had an old-fashioned ambiance to it, with brown hardwood floors and tanned walls that needed to be repainted. The table was round and small but perfect for two people.

"I heard you were back," someone came up from behind and brushed his hand over her shoulder. "Come on. Give me a hug."

Boyd stood an even six feet with a brawny build. He now had a small gut, his football days behind him. He was also her ex-boyfriend and the last boy she ever dated before leaving for college.

Sky stood and welcomed him with an embrace that lasted longer than she cared for. He was friendly but she remembered Boyd had been too immature for his years. But that was high school, and she didn't want to let that be how she saw him now.

"I heard you moved away," Sky asked, making conversation.

He nodded. "Yep. Became a realtor and living my dream life," he smiled and looked her over. "You are as beautiful as the last time I saw you," he acknowledged. "I'm in town to visit my parents until New Years and I heard you'd been back almost two weeks now."

"Something like that," Sky admitted. "Came for my dad."

Boyd nodded. "That's what I heard." His smile widened as if seeing his future suddenly and Sky groaned.

When she'd come out to her dad, she was in college and Boyd was gone. She wondered if someone relayed to him at some point that she was gay.

"So, look, I'd love to have dinner with you some time. Catch up on life," he said.

One of his friends, someone Sky recognized from childhood walked up and patted him on the back.

"Boyd." He shook his head.

Boyd looked confused and exchanged looks from Sky to his friend. His bushy brows knitted together. "What am I missing?" He looked down at her hand to check for a wedding ring and said, "are you seeing someone?"

"No, but..."

"Then perfect." He cut her off.

Sky mentally groaned. He still hadn't broken the habit of cutting her off. That was their entire relationship in high school. Sky smirked and picked up her mug to salute him.

"I'm a lesbian," she stated with content.

To say his mouth hung open was an understatement. He stared shocked, as if a woman like her couldn't be gay. His friend laughed and reached over to close his mouth.

Boyd shrugged him away.

"Umm." He looked uncomfortable and confused.

Sky could see him working out how she could be a lesbian when they dated but she wouldn't help him figure that out. They had never slept together but had kissed dozens of times, all while Sky mentally timed when they would end.

Right on time, Maxine walked up and grinned.

"Hey, Boyd." She noticed his stunned look and frowned. "What's wrong with him?" she asked.

Boyd's friend laughed. "He just realized his dreams weren't all going to come true." With that, he guided Boyd away and Sky turned and snorted, unable to hide her laughter.

"What did I miss?" Maxine asked, not wanting to be left out.

"You missed me telling him that I'm gay," Sky said, eyes tearing up at how ridiculously hurt Boyd looked.

"Damn," Maxine complained. "And you couldn't wait until I got here to do that?"

Sky rolled her eyes. "Sorry! Next time I have to disappoint someone, I'll delay the inevitable."

"Thank you," Maxine smirked.

Sky shoved her friend playfully and reached for her drink. It had cooled enough for her to drink without burning her tongue. She held it up and Maxine took hers.

"To the queer women of this town!"

"I'll cheers to that," Maxine said.

Their mugs clinked and they drank.

Maxine put her mug down.

"You said something about your plans for tomorrow changing. How so?"

Straight to the point. Sky was nervous.

"My dad has pretty much banned me from staying with him all day tomorrow."

"Oh." Maxine smiled. "You should have seen that coming. You are more than welcome to join us for Christmas."

"I know but I already found somewhere else I'm going."

"Oh, where?"

Sky sucked in a breath. "Eva's."

Maxine looked surprised and didn't bother trying to hide it.

"Eva's… yeah. Um. Her place is amazing."

Sky felt uncomfortable.

"You know what, I can just text her and say I'm spending Christmas with you guys."

"What?" Maxine disagreed, confounded by Sky's willingness to cancel on her behalf. "No!" Maxine waved her hands and exhaled sharply. "I'm fine."

"I know, but… you two still have some things… to sort through. And you are non-monogamous, so… I don't know." For all Sky knew, Maxine still harbored feelings for Eva.

Maxine laughed. "Yes, we are. But James and I only go out and meet individuals together, for an occasional third, and definitely outside of this town."

Sky nodded. Maybe she was overthinking things.

"I still care about Eva and that will never change. Our time was brief but impactful. I'm confident, now that you've opened her up, we'll have the conversation we need to let things go and even become friends."

"I just want to respect our friendship above all else," Sky admitted.

"But why?" Maxine brows furrowed. "You two are only becoming friends and she's not your type, as you've pointed out more than once."

"I haven't…" Sky shut her mouth and picked up her mug to take a drink. Maxine was right. Sky made it clear Eva was not someone she could be into.

"But…" Maxine waited until Sky looked up to listen. "If you ever did realize… you wanted more from her, I would be fine with that. I'd actually hope for it."

"Maxine…" Sky whined, over being told how she might feel for someone else, as if she needed assistance.

"I'm just saying," Maxine pointed out. "High school was over ten years ago, and I hate how shallow we were as kids to not notice her before that night. She's amazing and deserves to finally be happy in this town. Even if that's just making a bunch of friends."

Maxine was speaking of the night half the graduating class watched as Eva's personal life was exposed, humiliating her. It still haunted Sky, how no teachers held the ones responsible for that night accountable.

"Hey. Let's enjoy tonight and tomorrow, let it bring us whatever joy may come." Maxine held her mug up for the second time and Sky nodded as she joined in the toast.

Sky could worry about her new friendship with Eva tomorrow. Tonight was all about living in the now.

*

"How's my girl this morning?" Sky's dad extended his arm out as she went in for a hug.

Sky could see how healthy her dad looked compared to many of the patients in the neighboring rooms and counted her blessings that he'd make a full recovery. He had shaved recently and was wearing his clothes when she arrived. He looked ready for a party but seeing him lying in a bed with rails to prevent him from falling reminded her of how much progress he still needed to make.

"I'm good, Dad." She took a seat beside him. "You are looking sharp."

"I told you. I have some friends coming by in another hour." He reached for the mug on his moving tray that was propped in front of him, removing the tea bag from the mug. "You look nice."

Sky had on some jeans, Uggs, and a blouse, feeling comfortable and ready for an unexpected day at Eva's home. She'd twisted her dreads into a design that swooped to one side, her edges slick and styled.

"Thanks," she said.

She waited for him to say more, as was his usual habit, but he only focused on his tea.

Sky narrowed her eyes, waiting for him to smile and finally make a comment about spending time with Eva but it never came. What was he planning? It no longer mattered when Eva walked in, wearing a Christmas sweater that Sky would have never been caught wearing and a beanie that matched its disastrous look. There were white fuzzy balls on the beanie and sweater that Sky assumed to be snowballs. Instead of a Santa stitched on the front of the sweater, it was a younger version of a Mrs. Claus and a female elf as they rode on a sled.

The more Sky studied the sweater the more she saw the humor and appeal. Eva was unique and despite being awkward around people, she did not try to hide her personality with the sweaters she wore. Half the time she either looked like a tech nerd or an unstylish reclusive woman. But during their few encounters, Sky had come to see that Eva had no problem being honest or expressing herself.

Would Sky have walked up to Eva or considered being friends with her in high school? Unfortunately, she already knew the answer as they had never shared a moment in all their years attending the same schools.

Sky watched Eva saunter over and could feel her dad's eyes pinned on her. Sky shifted slightly so he couldn't look at her face. She wanted to hide behind a rock, aware her dad could tell what she had been thinking.

"How are you feeling?" Eva asked Sky's dad as he gestured for her to move the tray.

"Better than I was yesterday," he answered.

Eva held up a small, wrapped gift.

"Merry Christmas."

Sky's dad examined the box and his eyes lit up as he tore the paper away to reveal a jewelry box. Sky watched as her dad opened it to find a pocket watch inside. He blew out a breath and shook his head, fighting back tears. Sky stared, amazed by the joy that emanated from her dad over a pocket watch and wanted to know why he'd become so touched by the gift.

He picked up the pocket watch, the chain dangling around his fingers as he opened it.

"You remembered?" he asked Eva.

Eva nodded. "It took some doing but after my investigation, I found out who bought it and after some bargaining, they gave it to me. I also got it restored."

"What is it?" Sky asked. She needed to know what was so special about the watch.

Her dad held it up and turned it to the back. Engraved on it were her dad and mom's initials. Sky looked confused.

"Years ago, your mom bought this for me and engraved it. It held so much sentimental value. But we had our financial struggles and I had to pawn it one year to pay the bills. It was a hard thing to do but your mom and I hoped I'd be able to get it back one day. When the time came… the pawn shop had sold it, and we could never find the buyer." Sky's dad looked at Eva in amazement. "How did you find it?"

"I created a promo commercial post across social media until someone who used to live here responded. It took almost two months but once they confirmed that they had it, all that was left was to retrieve it." Eva had gone out her way to find something of value to Sky's dad and acted as if that was something anyone would do.

Sky studied Eva and wondered how someone like her could exist. She had remembered her dad mentioning a pocket watch in a story he told her once years ago, but she never thought anything of it.

"You are something special," he said.

Eva smiled and averted her head, not comfortable with the compliment.

"Okay. Enough." He huffed and waved for them to leave. "Go and have fun today. And make sure you bring me back leftovers."

Eva chuckled. "I actually left cookies and food with the nurses. They want you to follow the regimen that the doctor has given you, and then they'll bring it to you later today."

"You should have snuck it in here," he complained.

"No, she shouldn't have," Sky said sternly.

He grumbled in disapproval.

"Alright. Leave me to my misery."

"You're so dramatic," Sky teased.

"Get going," he said, banishing them away.

Eva looked up. "Ready."

Sky looked to her dad and nodded.

"Yes." She leaned down and kissed his forehead. "I'll come visit in the morning."

"Yay," he mumbled and turned on the television.

Nothing else left to say, they left.

*

After Eva's suggestion to Sky leave her car at her dad's house, she'd hopped into Eva's car to head to her house. She lived on the border of town and up toward the mountains, where snow lightly fell. It wasn't too much to be concerned about, but Sky wasn't used to driving in snow so she was relieved by Eva's experience.

It took almost thirty minutes to reach her house, the rural area filled with weaving roads and no streetlights. It was almost eleven in the morning and Sky wondered how they'd fill the time. She'd never spent the holidays with anyone but her family, close friends, or an ex's family.

They passed other homes that were spaced apart, giving each other enough privacy. When Eva pulled up to her home, Sky stared out the window stunned by the beauty.

Eva's home was surrounded with trees and a trail that went into the woods. Her rustic cabin home was two stories high with large windows all along the front of the house, on both levels. The cabin was made of wood, stone, and other natural materials that featured simple but elegant designs. Her porch stretched across the front of the house with a swinging bench off to the side.

Eva parked in front and turned off her car.

"Ready to go inside."

It took Sky a moment, eyes wide as she let out a breath.

"Wow. You live here?" She pointed to the house as if there had been some mistake and they'd ended up at the wrong home.

Eva smiled. "Yeah. I bought it from this older couple three years ago. I've made some upgrades and created a trail through the back that leads to a creek. Come on. Let me show you around."

Eva climbed out of the car and Sky followed, still amazed. They walked along the side of the house, a path leading to the back as Eva pointed out the changes she had made.

It was a large backyard that was fenced in with a gate leading to the trail she had created.

"This actually used to be overrun with bushes, but I cleared it to make a backyard. I own about a half-acre in total but all I need is this."

The back of the home didn't have an entrance.

"In the next year I plan to extend this part of the house and create a back deck."

"Eva, this is beautiful." Sky felt herself wanting to give her a hug, but she stopped herself.

"Thank you. Come on. It's getting cold out here." Eva directed them back to the front of the house and unlocked the door as they stepped inside.

The inside was warm and inviting, the smell of cookies and other delicious foods floating in the air. Eva walked over to a fireplace and placed a log inside, as she opened the chute and started a fire.

Sky walked around the living room, admiring the chandelier hovering over the couch. Eva's home had a warm glow of burgundy and blue throughout with hardwood floors.

Maxine had said Eva's home was amazing, but she had understated its beauty. Sky had always pictured having a home like this but thought it was something only people in movies could experience.

"Are you thirsty?" Eva asked. It had been a long time since she invited someone new to her home.

Sky hadn't realized Eva was beside her and looked toward the kitchen.

"Oh, water would be great."

"Coming up."

Sky followed Eva into the kitchen, the design of the home more of the same, her cabinets painted a royal blue with granite marble countertops that gave a modern ambiance. There was an island at the center with a farmhouse kitchen sink.

Eva grabbed two glasses from the cabinet, poured water from a pitcher in the fridge and handed one to her.

"Thank you."

Eva nodded. "I thought you might like to take a walk before it gets cold and check out the creek." She noticed Sky's brow raise and smiled. "It's not a hike, I promise. It'll take less than five minutes to get there, and the view is beautiful."

"Sounds like a good idea," Sky agreed.

"Cool." They walked back to the front door and Eva turned, scrutinizing Sky's appearance and frowned. "Umm. One second."

Sky watched Eva disappear around a corner that was along the stairs and walk back with a coat that looked fuzzy and warm.

"It can get cold up this way." She held it out for Sky to slide her arms through.

Sky moved forward and allowed Eva to assist her in putting the coat on. She turned to face Eva, comfortably snug in the coat. Sky nervously looked away, frowning, self-conscious of her reaction.

Sky stared off to a random area and smiled.

"Thank you."

"Of course. I can't have you returning to your dad sick," Eva joked.

"I doubt you could ever do anything wrong in my dad's eyes," Sky admitted.

Eva only smiled and opened the door. She waved for Sky to walk out first and followed behind.

They walked silently side by side until they heard the sound of flowing water nearby.

Eva pointed ahead.

"It's just around the corner."

Once they reached the creek, Sky looked forward, surface water flowing toward the nearest river. There were large to small sized rocks stacked throughout the creek with a small three-foot waterfall further along the path.

"There's actually a water hole a half mile down. It's large enough for two people to soak in," Eva said, pointing downstream.

"This is all yours?" Sky asked in disbelief.

Eva nodded. There was a small open shed to their right where she stored a small bag filled with essentials, wood covered with a tarp, and a sleeping bag.

"You camp out here?" Sky asked.

"Yeah. Mostly during fall and summer. It's beautiful out here during that time."

"What about black bears or cougars?" Sky couldn't picture being out here, exposed to all the elements and wildlife.

"I manage. Besides, as long as I keep a fire going and make noise, that's usually half the battle."

Sky snorted. "Right." She turned back to the water and sighed. "This is beautiful. You are very lucky."

It took Eva a minute to respond. She grabbed two chairs and offered one to Sky as they sat.

"I'm grateful to have a home like this."

Sky was relieved Eva had offered her the coat and slid her hands into the pockets. There was a lot about Eva that Sky didn't know. She smiled when the sun peeked through the trees and laminated the creek.

"How long were you in foster care?"

Eva hadn't expected that question. She shifted her beanie lower and contemplated her response.

Sky immediately regretted her question.

"Sorry. I shouldn't have assumed you'd want to share something like that with me." She chuckled awkwardly. "I guess you're right. I have a habit of being persistent with inquisitions." She looked at Eva and sighed. "I just... find myself admiring you more every day, and I want to know your story. Not to be nosy... but because... I care."

It was easy to believe but it was still hard to open up. Eva said she'd try harder and that could only happen if she talked. "I went into the system at nine. My mom died giving birth to me, so it was always just me and my dad. Until he passed."

Sky noticed Eva's hesitation and thought better than to ask how he died.

"No other family?"

Eva shook her head. "At least none mentioned." Eva found herself feeling brave enough to share more. "My dad did have a sister, but they were estranged, and I never met her. But he never felt alone or isolated back then. I was his whole world, and he was mine."

"Sounds like my dad," Sky whispered.

Eva nodded. "My dad was a quiet man, but he spoke loudly through his actions and love for nature. We had a home similar to the one I have now."

"Did you ever have foster parents?" Sky remembered their graduation but didn't recall seeing anyone celebrating Eva's accomplishments.

"Many, but at the end, I was in a group home until I left for college at 18."

"Oh. I assumed you stayed here." Sky couldn't picture Eva in a big city.

"I was gone for two years. I thought if I left... my past would not follow." Eva snorted and leaned into the chair. "I was very wrong about that. I came back, pursued my master's in software engineering and during that time fell in love with graphic design and product building and the rest is history."

"So, you're also a software engineer?" Sky asked, wanting to give the woman a medal of honor. Eva held so many accomplishments and she wanted to know her secret to success.

"Yeah, but I hardly use it." Eva offered Sky some M&M's.

"Thanks." Sky held her hand out and popped one in her mouth when Eva poured her a handful.

"Costume cosmetic artist. That's not something you hear people pursuing every day. Tell me, why that?" Eva stretched her legs out and linked her fingers in front of her.

Sky blushed, shy to talk about it. There wasn't much she could say compared to the success Eva had in her career. People assumed she was doing well but really, Sky had been merely trying to survive lately.

"Well… I haven't actually done much with it other than small gigs here and there. As a kid I loved watching movies and seeing the way characters changed. And when Chas got into theater, seeing firsthand how it all worked, transforming people's looks and making them look like an entirely different person, it all thrilled me."

"I like that." Eva closed her eyes and soaked in the moment. She didn't think it would be this easy to connect with Sky, let alone be comfortable enough to have her in her home. Eva wanted to get to know her without the pressure of her friends, and without expectations.

Sky turned and found herself staring at Eva, who was completely unaware. Eva's head was tilted back, highlighting her long neck and sharply angular jaw.

Hmm.

Eva was never easy to read. She didn't fit any lesbian stereotypical box, and she certainly had her own style, somewhat bohemian. Maxine was right to say that Eva was beautiful. Unique, androgynous, and striking. Even her voice was smooth and rich, leaving Sky wanting to close her eyes every time the woman talked.

Eva turned and opened her eyes to find Sky staring. She straightened up.

"Uh… ready to head back?"

Sky stood and shut her eyes, embarrassed to be caught. She swallowed and nodded as Eva put the chairs away and guided them back to the house.

Sky walked quietly as Eva brought up ideas of what they could do today. When they reached the house, Eva escorted them inside and kicked off her boots.

"I'm going to change into something more comfortable. Feel free to look around," Eva announced.

Sky stood in between the living space and kitchen and watched Eva head up toward a room in the back. She exhaled and turned toward the fireplace, seeing small, framed artwork propped on the floating shelves above.

There were no pictures on the walls to show the people who mattered to Eva over the years or small trinket gifts to show the adventures she'd experienced. Her home was a home without anyone to share it with.

It wasn't Sky's place to question Eva, but she hoped that they could have a friendship one day.

Chapter Twelve

"These cookies are so good!" Sky moaned with her feet tucked underneath her on the couch.

Eva sat on the other side, legs stretched across the ottoman, and grabbed another gingerbread cookie from the tray that sat between them. They'd spent several hours watching Christmas movies, and playing board and video games, before eating dinner.

"You are free to take as many cookies as you like home with you," Eva offered. "And leftovers."

Sky moaned into another bite and rolled her eyes back, raptured in the cookie.

"Do not tempt me." She took her time chewing, leaning into the cushions. "I haven't had a dinner like this since my mom," Sky admitted. "Thanks for everything."

It was almost eight and they'd lost track of time. Eva couldn't remember a moment when she was swept away by another person's presence. She never envisioned herself sitting across the couch from Sky Wyman, their lives never aligning, before now. Eva's initial fear had been replaced by the possibilities of future interactions.

Another twenty minutes and the lesbian movie *I Hate New Years* ended. Sky stretched out her arms, ready to climb into a bed. She reached around for her phone, unable to find it and smiled, sated by the day she had spent.

Eva tilted her head, keen to see Sky content and comfortable in her home.

"You're smiling."

Sky pursed her lips to one side, grin widening.

"Yeah. This was… unexpected."

"Did you think I'd be tucked in a corner somewhere, playing with a pet lizard or something?" Eva asked jokingly.

Sky narrowed her eyes, aware that Eva was joking and laughed.

"No!" She rolled her eyes. "But I will admit… I thought you'd find it hard to talk to me."

Eva nodded, understanding Sky's initial concern coming here.

"I like talking to you," Eva admitted.

There was silence and Eva looked up, suddenly worried she'd said too much. She sucked in a breath and smiled timidly.

"Umm. I'm glad you came. I have hesitated to take risks with people. Meeting you… during this phase of our life has been worth every experience."

"Good! And I like talking to you too!" Sky smiled.

Eva stood and stretched.

"I'll take you home."

Sky shook her head.

"You don't have to do that. I can request a Lyft."

"Yeah… that's not likely to happen." Eva headed toward the kitchen, calling from behind. "I'll put some leftovers and more cookies in a container, and we can head out."

"Okay." Sky found herself not wanting to leave but what else would she do, spend the night? Their friendship was not there yet, and it was getting late.

Eva held up the bag of food for Sky when she walked toward the door. Sky's shoes were on, and she had her purse tucked to her side.

"Here you go."

"Thanks."

"One sec," Eva bent down to put on her boots.

Sky glanced down, eyes on Eva's ass and shook her head, turning away.

"What am I doing?"

"Huh?" Eva twisted her head up to look at Sky, tying her shoelaces.

Sky hadn't meant to say anything and shrugged.

"Oh nothing. Talking to myself."

Eva heard what Sky said but wouldn't think too much about it, since it wasn't meant for her to hear. Today had been revealing and Eva wanted to think about what kind of friendship she wanted to have with Sky and if she was ready to bring herself out of hiding. As Eva guided them to her car, she felt candid joviality for the first time in her life. The kind that left her excited to see Sky again and during the drive back, Eva found herself smiling.

*

Eva sat in her usual spot at the coffee shop, hunched over her laptop. She had sworn not to add on extra work until after the New Year but was pulled in by her inability to ignore people who needed her help. She'd taken on a new client and planned to rebuild their website after the holidays, only to learn the day after Christmas that their website had been hacked.

Two days later, Eva was still staring at the chaos of the website and seeing how terribly built it was by the previous designers. They'd cut corners and it was disheartening to learn how much money her new client spent on the website before reaching out to her.

It was midday and she hadn't taken a break since the morning.

Eva heard someone approach and looked up, a burning ache in her eyes from staring at the screen too long. Maxine stood with a mug and a ham and cheese croissant. Eva massaged her temple and straightened.

"Uh... hey," Eva said, trying not to be weird.

Maxine smiled. "Hi." Her gaze wavered but she found the confidence to look back at Eva's contemplative stare. "You've hardly touched your tea and I wanted to bring you a fresh mug and something to eat. My treat."

Eva couldn't remember the last time they'd had a genuine conversation or an attempt at one. Their past had been brief, but it stung and left a rift between them that eventually dissolved into mutual evasion.

Eva looked down at the cold tea she'd unintentionally neglected and smiled.

"Thanks." She closed her laptop and moved it to the side, making room. "I guess I lost track of time."

"Everything okay?" Maxine placed the mug and plate on the table.

"I had an unexpected issue with a new client and I'm trying to figure out how to salvage their site, but I know damn well that I'll need to start from scratch. I ran a diagnostic and because my client used an insecure site through Wordpress; the only thing I can do now is check if their backup files were affected." She was exhausted about the amount of time it would take to rebuild her client's website. She'd initially gone into the contract with the false illusion that all she'd need to do was redesign the website, and now it would take months and lots of money on her client's end to do what was needed.

Eva picked up the mug and breathed the aroma of honey and peppermint.

"This will help. Thanks again."

Eva expected Maxine to leave but she was still standing there. Eva knew she could take the opportunity to make the first move and invite Maxine to sit. If Eva wanted to continue to build a friendship with Sky, she needed to finally squash the past between her and Maxine. But Eva could also admit, through their brief time together, she enjoyed Maxine's presence and missed it. They'd never taken the chance to become friends.

"Would you… umm… like to sit?" Eva asked, her fingers digging into her thighs.

Maxine's smile reached her eyes.

"Yeah." She pulled out the chair and sat down.

For the longest minute, they sat in silence, neither one of them ready to talk. The initial awkwardness passed, and Eva felt strangely comfortable sitting across from Maxine.

"I never said sorry for hurting you," Maxine rushed out. She held her hand out, gesturing as if to assist in pacing herself. "I'm sorry. I should have… at the very least explained why I wanted to keep what we had to ourselves."

Eva listened, not angry or sad about the outcome of their brief affair. It had been a couple of years and without realizing it, she'd let a lot go. For Eva, it was trusting that it was safe to open herself up to someone again.

"I haven't been mad about it in a long time. I didn't understand but... after a while, I thought about who I'd gotten to know. That Maxine wouldn't have kept our connection secret out of embarrassment for liking me." Eva sighed and smiled. "That's why I've been coming to your coffee shop. Not to support a local business but to support you specifically."

A tear fell from Maxine's eye, and she nodded.

"I felt awake for the first time in a long time when we were together. At that time, I was afraid of coming out to my parents. I'd been suppressing my sexuality for years. That's one of the reasons why I moved away, like so many of us do as queer people in a town," Maxine explained.

Eva regretted not asking more questions. She'd assumed the worst and not considered any other options for Maxine's need to maintain discretion.

"I'm sorry that I let my insecurities get in the way. I didn't give you the time or space to explain and chose to run."

Maxine smiled. "I'm happy that we are talking now. I've missed you." She hesitated but reached across the table to link their fingers. "Can we start over?"

Eva considered how it would look to be Maxine's friend. She'd moved on and what feelings she had before no longer took place in her heart. Maxine was sweet, supportive, and easy to talk to. Eva noticed a few of the regular customers watching them and she exhaled. The awkwardness was Eva's own doing, not the people around her. If anything, they were curious but if she took a breath long enough, maybe one day it would be natural for her to interact with others.

Eva nodded. "I'd like that."

"Damn!" Maxine straightened, relieved that Eva wanted to reciprocate the chance to be friends. "I love this."

They sat staring at each other, not sure of what to say next, when they heard someone clear their throat.

Maxine moved her hand away and Eva did the same thing. Maxine glanced up and smiled at Sky standing beside them.

"Hey, I didn't know you were coming by."

"I uh, wanted to catch up. I've been spending time with my dad the last few days and I missed you." Sky's voice was soft, casually glancing at Eva before looking back at Maxine impassively.

Eva kept her eyes down at the table, incapable of explaining what she and Maxine had been talking about. Her phone buzzed and she checked the text. Denise and Sabrina were group chatting her and wanted to schedule a hang out. She texted back, ignoring the conversation Maxine and Sky were having.

When Eva was finished with her text, Maxine was standing.

"Duty calls," Maxine said, relaxed for the first time in a long time in Eva's presence. "I appreciate you and… let's do this again."

Eva nodded. "Thank you for coming to talk to me."

Maxine walked away and it was Sky's turn to sit down, her eyes scrutinizing every inch of Eva's face. Her jaw clenched for only a second before letting out a breath.

"I haven't seen you since Christmas. I was beginning to worry."

Eva's instinct was to become guarded, unsure of what Sky would say. It took Eva a second to remind herself that they were on good terms and there was nothing to be worried about.

"I had a work emergency come up right after Christmas and I've been dealing with that ever since," Eva explained.

"Oh." Sky looked around, finding Maxine at the register, a lot of thoughts going through her mind.

Eva could tell something was bothering Sky and was tempted to address what Sky had walked in on. But Eva couldn't see why Sky would be bothered by that and dismissed the thought. Besides, Maxine would most likely tell her anyway.

Whatever was bothering Sky seemed to pass as she smiled and tapped her fingertips playfully on the table.

"Have you given Chas's offer any thought?"

"Umm…" Eva had been too swamped with work to be thinking about the high school theater program.

"Eva!" Sky grumbled, sagging into the chair. "I know that you'd love it."

Eva's brows furrowed, not optimistic about that. One thing was for certain, Eva loved Sky's pouty expression. One corner of Eva's face turned up into a smile. It was small but she felt it.

"Can you swear to that?" Eva challenged.

"I mean." Sky's nose squinted as she hunched her shoulders. "You have a seventy percent chance at not regretting the decision to join in on the fun. And ninety, if you actually allow yourself to enjoy it."

"What about having a one-hundred percent chance? I'm a hundred or nothing at all, kind of person." Eva found herself relaxed, aware of being out in the open for people to see and judge. She always controlled how much she wanted others to see, and no one saw her laugh. She was emotionally exposed for the first time in years, and it felt strange and *out of body.*

Sky pursed her lips and rolled her eyes.

"The last ten would be you simply getting to work beside me."

Eva frowned and studied Sky with curiosity. Was Sky flirting with her? Eva shrugged away the thought, reading too much into it. The woman beside her was Sky Wyman. A woman who would never look at Eva in any way other than friends, and they were barely becoming that.

Eva did find working with Sky appealing and could see their collaboration being picturesque.

"I'd say, working with you would be worth more than ten percent. But..."

"No buts." Sky reached across the table and squeezed Eva's hand. "Do you really want to make me beg?" Sky asked. "Let showing this town your talent be at the top of your New Year's resolution."

Eva groaned. "I have a lot on my plate."

"If you don't want to do it... you know the words to say." Sky leaned back and waited for Eva to speak.

Eva took the moment to digest her feelings. She couldn't ignore the choices she needed to make. She didn't normally procrastinate but she also never put herself in a position that would make her uncomfortable. She always avoided options like that.

Eva was not the same girl from high school and the kids at the school weren't the classmates she had experienced. She was safe and no one could take away her happiness and it was time to face herself and be brave.

"I have zero desire to be at every function or participate in any way, other than as an artist and graphic designer."

"Okay." Sky's smile was contagious.

"Shouldn't you run this by Chas before agreeing to my terms?" Eva asked.

Sky laughed. "It's no surprise to me that you want to stick to the bare minimum. And he doesn't expect anything more than what you just said."

Eva groaned. "Why am I about to agree to this?" she mumbled, shaking her head.

"Because I'm hard to resist," Sky teased.

Sky's words sent an involuntary shiver down Eva's back. It was not hard to believe that statement in every context of the words.

"Fine. I'll do it," Eva stated.

Sky squealed, jolting in excitement.

"You are amazing. Chas will be so happy to hear."

There was no going back, and Eva wouldn't. She wasn't a fan of breaking promises or commitments and she'd hate to see the disappointment on Sky's face. She wanted to see her new friend in the making happy, and in return, it uplifted her mood.

Eva began to put her stuff away and looked at Sky, who watched her intensely. Again, Sky had a look in her eyes Eva couldn't comprehend but she said nothing. She stood and pulled her backpack on.

"I'll come by to see your dad tomorrow."

"Cool." Sky stood up too.

Eva nodded, sensing a nervous energy in Sky, and smiled as if that would help whatever was bothering her. It seemed to work; Sky smiled back.

"I'll send you my email. Feel free to pass it along to Chas."

"Okay." Sky seemed to rely on a one-word response and a smile.

"Good night," Eva said.

Sky nodded and whispered, "Night."
Eva left without saying another word.

Chapter Thirteen

Sky helped Maxine close, the last customer leaving just after nine. She had a lot to process and was painfully aware of Eva noticing her bizarre change of behavior. She couldn't say what had exactly caused her to react differently but the underlining thing she couldn't stop thinking about was what she walked had in on.

Deep down, Sky knew she was overreacting to potentially nothing. But still, finding them with hands embraced, staring at each other in silence, Sky felt a ping of jealousy. At what, she had no clue. It wasn't her business to ask, and Eva didn't owe it to her to bring it up.

"You've been wiping the same spot for almost two minutes." Maxine was standing beside her and reached for the towel.

Sky handed it over and sat in the chair closest to her.

"If this is about what you saw earlier, I told you… I've moved on. We were merely taking the moment we never had before to finally let things go and move forward." Maxine sat beside Sky, not wanting to be misunderstood.

Sky waved and spoke sincerely.

"Oh, I know. I was curious but that was just me being me."

One of Maxine's brows arched dubiously.

"Then why the face?"

Sky sighed. "I find myself saying silly or just inappropriate things to Eva and I don't understand why I'm acting that way." Sky hadn't known what she'd say or how true her words would be, until she'd sais them aloud. She knew how crazy she sounded. She was always in control of what came out of her mouth but as of late she'd lacked that control.

"Well…" Maxine could say a lot but knew it wouldn't be what Sky wanted to hear, so she chose an easier explanation. "Eva is easy to talk to. She can make you feel like you're the only one in the room."

Sky noticed the tenderness in Maxine's voice and how much she valued Eva by the depth of her emotion reflected in her eyes. She studied her friend and reached across the table.

"You loved her?"

Maxine smiled weakly.

"I was falling. I don't think it's wrong to miss that part of myself… when I was with her. James is well aware. It's being okay with loving more than one person. That we both believe in that makes our relationship work." Maxine noticed Sky's surprised reaction and shook her head to clarify. "I will always love Eva in my own way, but we're the past and I've been okay with that."

Sky chuckled. "Does that woman even know how attractive and amazing she is?"

A smile crept over Maxine's face; brows lifted in curiosity.

"Oh, so now she's attractive?" she teased.

"I never said she wasn't," Sky argued. "She's… attractive in a different way."

"Oh. Okay!" Maxine was still smiling.

"Don't do that," Sky quipped. She leaned into the chair and crossed one leg over the other. "I think Eva's awesome. I have not denied that. She's just… different."

"Maybe different is what you need," Maxine mumbled under her breath.

Sky would not entertain that with a response.

"Anyway. She agreed to work with me and Chas for the play coming up."

"Really?" Maxine smiled. "I'm so happy that she's finally coming out of her shell. She needs this."

Sky agreed with that. Feeling better after their conversation, she straightened.

"Okay. Let's finish closing so we can go get a drink."

Maxine grinned. She was happy to have Sky home and tried not to count the days until she left again. For now, Maxine would enjoy every moment with her friend and, just maybe, watch Sky do something different and out of her comfort zone.

She stood and pulled out her phone.

"I'll text James, and I'll be all yours."

*

Sky had seen Eva a few times over the next few days, while they were both visiting her dad. New Year's Eve was tonight, and she had plans to meet Maxine, James, and Chas at the bar in an hour to celebrate.

Sky walked into the room to find Eva and her dad playing a game of chess. They were immersed in the game, neither cracking a smile as Sky's dad studied the chessboard before reaching in to move a piece. Sky watched from the doorway as Eva sneakily grinned.

"Son of a bitch," Sky's dad grumbled. He had actively admitted on several occasions that he was a sore loser.

He moved his king in an attempt to defend against Eva, and she moved to take his pawn, only to force another grumble out of him. After a few more rounds, Eva forced a checkmate and won the game.

"I've been cooped up in a bed for weeks now. When I'm better... we'll see who will be winning." Sky's dad loved to trash talk.

"I'll give you a few more weeks of recovery," Eva joked.

Her dad huffed dramatically, looking down at the chess board in annoyance.

It was Sky's perfect time to announce herself.

"Alright, now. We don't need you working yourself up."

"What am I going to do? Leap out of bed to throttle her for winning?" he retorted.

Eva laughed and scooted her chair back to gain some distance from Sky's dad.

"Maybe," she joked.

He lifted his hands out, preferring not to be double-teamed.

"Fine. I'll accept the loss, for now."

"You have no choice," Eva teased.

Sky's dad gave her a warning glare and Sky did the same.

"Don't go antagonizing him. Goodness." She found Eva smiling and it touched Sky to see it. There was a glow in her eyes Sky had only noticed on rare occasions.

"Are you going to come over here and give me a proper greeting or shall I wait?" He had noticed his daughter staring at Eva, a smirk plastered over her face.

Sky squinted her eyes at her dad and walked over to hug him.

"Hey, Dad." She looked at Eva and smiled. "Hey. I was hoping to catch you here."

"Oh, yeah." Eva slid her hands into her coat pockets.

Sky nodded. Her dad studied her, and she twisted her body so he couldn't see her face and heard him chuckle lightly.

"We're celebrating New Year's Eve at the bar and uh... I know it's not your thing, but I wanted to ask anyway if you'd like to join us." She was speaking fast and holding her breath the entire time. When she inhaled it took her a second to release her breath; the tension in her chest had not gone away.

She had never felt nervous or shy around anyone at this magnitude before. She nibbled on her inner lip and frowned, not sure what to say next.

"Umm..." Eva hesitated and seemed out of place too.

"That sounds like a perfect idea. Eva was just sharing with me that she's never celebrated New Year's in a big way. Seems to me... now is your chance." Sky's dad stared at Eva and waited for her response.

Eva narrowed her eyes at him, suspiciously. She couldn't see herself spending New Year's Eve in a bar and with Sky and her friends, no less.

She considered how she could make this easier on herself.

"Can I invite a few friends?"

Sky was shocked that Eva was considering and responded quickly.

"Of course. The more, the merrier."

"I love this. My two favorite girls… spending the New Year's together." They both looked at him, neither saying a word, their narrowed expressions doing the talking.

*

"Happy New Year's Eve!" Maxine shouted. They'd gotten a large booth in the back, away from the band. The bar was packed with a lot of familiar faces. Sky pulled Maxine in for a hug.

"I see y'all started without me."

Chas handed Sky a shot of whiskey.

"Bitch, you were taking too long, and we have every intention of getting drunk tonight!"

They all laughed, and Sky downed her shot quickly, her shoulders already loosening.

"I invited Eva. I figured you wouldn't mind," Sky said, leaning toward Maxine who was already drinking another shot.

Maxine nodded and placed the glass on the table.

"Good. She's going to have fun and fit right in."

"She is bringing a few friends," Sky explained.

James nodded. "Most likely her ex, Denise and friend, Sabrina."

"Ex?" Sky asked inquisitively.

James nodded. "She doesn't think we know they dated but this is a small town, after all." He looked at his wife and laughed. "Well… some secrets do stay hidden on rare occasions."

Maxine rolled her eyes and looped her arms around his neck.

"Don't be a smart ass."

"Never…" he purred seductively. He wore black eyeliner and had slicked his hair back, wearing a black fishnet tank top and dark blue pants. His tanned skin glistened from the glitter splattered all over him.

They kissed and Sky rolled her eyes and looked at Chas, who was laughing. It wasn't often that James's feminine side flared but anytime he got handsy with Maxine and dressed more androgynously, she could see how open their relationship was. Not necessarily with them being non-monogamous but in their sexuality and relationship dynamic. They were both bisexual and Sky could imagine when they invited someone to their bedroom, they always ended the night fulfilled.

Sky wanted that. Not the poly lifestyle but being so in love, comfortable, and open with a person. The trust of knowing you could explore all your desires and never be shamed for them.

"Hey." Eva's voice was timid, but Sky heard it as if she'd whispered directly in her ear.

Sky turned and found herself smiling, happy to see Eva. It took her a second to process the shock racing through her body. Eva wasn't in her normal sweater or polo shirt. She still had her own unique style, but she also looked different.

There was no beanie to hide her perfect curly hair that was swept to one side. She wore no sweater to hide her toned, unmarked arms, that Sky had the privilege of feeling on both of the occasions when Eva had caught her. She wore a silky, multicolored, loose fitted short-sleeved shirt, with black skinny jeans and boots. Her scarf was gray with Star War characters on it.

Sky looked up into her light brown eyes. She hadn't noticed the depth of them until now. Eva also had one arrowhead earring dangling from her ear. She still looked nerdy but in a very sexy way. It threw Sky off and she didn't know what to say.

"Uh, hi!" Sky swallowed what felt like a lump in her throat. Her heart was pounding so fast.

Eva blushed and looked away, running her hand over the back of her neck.

"They wouldn't let me leave the house without getting dressed for the occasion." It was rare for Eva to dress up. The last time she'd put on clothes this formal was when she'd gone to a dance theater production a couple months ago, in a neighboring city.

"Uh… no…" Sky stuttered. Why was she acting so weird? She smiled and swallowed again.

"Hi." A woman in sparkling gold designer overalls and a black sports bra stepped to Eva's side and offered out a hand. "I'm Denise."

Sky accepted the handshake and snapped out of her daze.

"Hi. I'm Sky."

Maxine stepped forward and greeted Denise.

"We've met a few times in passing."

"Yeah. Maxine, right?" Denise asked politely.

"Yep." Maxine grinned. "Hey, Sabrina."

"What's up. I love your outfit," Sabrina complimented.

Sky remembered Sabrina from high school. They were never in the same social group growing up, but people knew Sabrina through her popularity as an athlete.

Maxine gave Eva an appraising look.

"You look… wow." She bumped her shoulder into Sky and grinned. "Right, Sky?"

Maxine was going to get an earful later. Sky gritted down the words she wanted to say to Maxine and smiled at Eva, who looked unsure of what to do.

"You look really nice." Sky was panicking, trying not to say the wrong thing.

Eva smiled and nodded.

"You do too."

James curled his arms around Maxine and nuzzled his nose into the crook of her neck.

"Let's go get another round of shots to celebrate our new friend's arrival."

"Sounds like a brilliant idea," Maxine agreed.

"We'll join you," Sabrina offered and looped her arm through Denise's to drag her with them.

Chas cleared his throat and pointed in a random direction, in an obvious attempt to give them privacy.

"I've been meaning to get close and personal with that fine ass man over there." He walked off.

Why were they treating them as if they were on a date? Sky was going to kill her friends later.

Eva stood, rocking on the balls of her feet with her hands hidden in her pockets.

"I know I look different. You can just say it," Eva said in a low voice.

Sky stared, confused. "Say what?"

Eva shrugged. "I don't know. That I don't look like me."

There was a lot Sky could say to that, but one thing came to mind.

"It *is* different but it's also still you."

"Really?" Eva seemed surprised by that.

"Of course. I still see the same unique, nerdy, understated attractive woman I've been getting to know." Sky wanted to pinch herself. Did she say that aloud?

Judging by Eva's widened eyes, she had.

Sky wanted to scream at herself for opening her big mouth again. She tried to change up the tone of conversation.

"I mean… Chas did say being a nerd was a compliment these days. I hope I didn't offend you."

Eva shook her head. "You haven't."

"Cool."

There was a long pause of silence before Eva asked, "I feel like I'm making you uncomfortable. We could just leave if you want."

"What? No! You're not," Sky promised.

"Then why do you keep frowning or looking as if you want to run?" Eva normally didn't ask blunt questions, but she'd seen enough of Sky's expressive looks to know this one was because of her.

Sky stepped forward and reached for Eva's hand, a rush of jitters causing goosebumps to form up her arm and back. She was feeling sensitive and shy as she answered.

"I promise you that I'm always happy to see you. I…"

"Here's your shot," Maxine offered.

Eva took a step back and turned to face her friends coming with shots in their hands. She smiled when Denise offered her one.

"Thanks."

Sky watched their interaction and found herself turning away. She felt a reluctance within herself and

126

wanted to run. Perhaps Eva was right to question her about how she felt now.

Sky relaxed when Maxine rubbed her back, soothing her like old times. Since they were kids, Maxine had always known when she was sad, upset, or lonely.

Sky forced a smile when James held his drink high, Chas coming with his own at the right moment.

"I'd like to toast to… challenging our paths in order to live our truths and sharing it with others." James's toast was an understatement.

Everyone cheered and drank in unison and whatever thoughts Sky had been feeling, she'd leave them for another day to figure out. Tonight, she'd have fun and spend it with the people who mattered.

Chapter Fourteen

A few hours later, Eva was just as uncomfortable as the instant she'd walked into the bar. Everyone seemed to be having fun while she just wanted to go home and watch a movie. Sabrina continued to hand her drinks that Eva would only give to Denise, not interested in being drunk.

It was a few minutes after eleven, the energy in the bar reaching a new level of excitement. Eva couldn't figure out what the big thrill was about starting a new year and celebrating it. Tomorrow would come, and it would be like any other day.

Someone bumped into her chair, smelling of alcohol and was too drunk to notice her. Eva wanted to bolt, more claustrophobic with every second that passed. She hardly ever came to bars and when she did, it was around six with only a few people inside. Usually, an older crowd.

Eva leaned in and whispered in Sabrina's ear that she was going outside for fresh air. She skirted around the tables, walking quickly to the exit, relieved the instant she could see the stars and feel the breeze. She took a breath and sighed.

What was she thinking, coming here, and acting like she could fit in? She checked the time on her wristwatch and looked off toward the road ahead. The temptation to leave was palpable but she'd never hear the end of it if she left, especially without saying goodbye.

Fifteen minutes passed and she felt no closer to going back inside.

A group of guys wobbled out of the bar, laughing uncontrollably. She stepped to the side before they bumped into her, unaware of her presence. That was nothing new to her.

One of the guys looked, eyes wide as he pointed at her with no coordination.

"You finally come out the cage," he said, his speech slurring.

Eva chose to ignore him, but he didn't leave. His friends stood there, confused until they finally acknowledged her.

"Hey, Eva…" Boyd smiled and patted one of his friends on the back.

She had to admit, she was surprised he knew her name. She couldn't remember the last time she saw him, and they'd never spoken before now. She nodded once.

"Hey man, she's the girl who used to wear these weird anime shirts and we thought was mute because she never spoke." Boyd's drunk friend staggered sloppily.

"Keith. Her name's Eva. Don't be a jackass." Boyd gave her a sympathetic smile.

Keith was the asshole's name. Eva remembered him back from high school but never cared to know his name. He was one of the people who used to bully her and still found himself funny.

Keith pointed rudely at Eva and laughed.

"Were you really hanging out with Boyd's ex-girlfriend? She's way too next level for most people in this damn town. Are you hoping for a miracle or something?"

He laughed as if that was the funniest idea he'd had all year.

Eva stared as if he was the biggest idiot in town.

"Last time you spoke to me… you thought it would be a great idea to take the gay out of me, remember? You thought I wanted to be gay because no boys thought I was special." He stared, dazed that she'd spoken back at all.

"I don't remember that," was the argument he wanted to go with.

"Well, I do," one of his friends said. "And it wasn't funny then and you aren't funny now."

Keith hissed. "She can handle it. She's a dyke."

"First, I was too frail to be seen. But now… what… I'm a dyke who's not cool enough to be with someone who you wouldn't be cool enough for even if she was straight?" Eva could see his cheeks reddening.

Keith stood there, dumbfounded and unable to say anything else.

Boyd and the others laughed at their friend.

"You deserved that, dumbass." Boyd nodded at Eva and shook his head. "I'm sorry he's still the same piece of shit he's always been. I'm embarrassed to be seen with him. I haven't been home and hung out with this idiot in a few years." Boyd looked awkward and uncomfortable, and she knew he was being honest.

It shouldn't have surprised Eva with how kind and supportive Boyd and the others were. They were all looking at Keith as if they couldn't wait to chastise him when he sobered up. Maybe coming out of hiding wouldn't be so bad after all. She'd defended herself and that was something she could never have done years ago. But even more, others stood up for her too.

The bar door opened, and Boyd looked up and smiled.

"We'll leave you two." Boyd assisted Keith to their car, the rest of them following and staggering along the sidewalk.

Eva turned to find Sky standing at the doorway, arms curled into herself, trying to suppress the cold. Sky smiled and walked toward Eva, wobbling a little. She was drunk but seemed relaxed and aware of where she was.

"I was looking for you. Everyone thought you went home," Sky said, speech a little slurred.

"I was planning to," Eva admitted.

"What happened?" she asked, her gaze on Boyd assisting Keith into the car.

Eva shrugged. "It doesn't matter." Eva wasn't mad but she didn't feel good either. Though she'd learned tonight that people had cared, she was also reminded of how much words could still hurt.

"It does… if it makes you look so sad." Sky reached out and brushed her fingertips over the corner of Eva's eye.

There was a desire deep within herself that wanted to lean into Sky's fingers and let it last longer, but the thought forced her to take a step back. She couldn't afford to feel any type of way toward Sky other than friendship. Sky was sweet and naturally affectionate, and Eva wouldn't read into that.

"I'm fine," Eva lied.

Sky studied her for the longest heartbeat until she stepped forward. Instinctively, Eva stepped back, and Sky groaned.

"I'm trying to comfort you. That's what friends do."

"Standing beside me is good enough," Eva said. She couldn't handle physical contact.

Sky frowned but didn't argue as they stood side by side.

A few minutes passed. Eva could see Sky shifting and she sighed.

"Are you cold?"

"Yeah," Sky admitted.

"You can go back inside. You don't have to stand out here with me."

"What if I'm staying because I don't want you to leave?" Sky's voice came out so soft and it confused Eva, causing her to turn and stare.

Eva couldn't read Sky's thoughts and by the awkward aversion of meeting her gaze it was obvious that Sky didn't know what she was trying to say either.

"Come on, you two." Maxine popped her head out from the bar. "The countdown is happening." She left without saying another word.

Sky reached for Eva's hand and linked their fingers to follow but Eva stood stiffly, like a rock unable to be moved.

Sky turned and looked perplexed.

"Eva. We have maybe a minute. You're telling me, you haven't had any fun at all?"

It was easy for Sky to fit in and go with the flow, surrounded by people. How could she understand how Eva felt? The last thing Eva wanted was to be a buzz kill and this was why she hesitated to come in the first place.

Eva shook her head. "Go in. I'll see you later." She let go of Sky's hand and as she turned to leave, was stunned when Sky grabbed her arm and moved to her side… a little too close.

"Sky…"

Her words were cut off by Sky's lips pressed against her own. Eva sucked in a breath, standing frozen in shock and unable to move. It took her a second and the sensation of Sky's tongue brushing against her lip before Eva could finally react. She planned to pull away but instead found herself moaning when she opened her mouth and felt Sky's tongue enter and lure her in as their kiss lingered.

Eva leaned in, ever so slightly, and felt Sky's fingers dig into her neck to pull her closer and they kissed again. The instant Eva's belly fluttered with desire that hadn't stirred in a long time, she finally snapped out of it and stepped back.

"We have to stop," Eva shook her head and waved her hand to prevent Sky from approaching. "You are drunk and would never do this if you weren't." Eva grimaced and wanted to be mad but knew she couldn't. How could she hold her accountable when this wasn't the rational Sky she'd gotten to know? "You probably won't even remember this." Eva laughed with no humor in her voice.

Sky seemed stunned by her own actions and was at a loss for words.

Eva was bemused and stared at Sky, annoyed that she'd given in for even a second.

"You would never have thought to kiss me if I looked like my casual self." She shook her head and heard everyone in the background shouting, '*Happy New Year!*'.

"I'm sorry." Sky's eyes watered.

All Eva could do was nod.

"I'll go." Sky looked at Eva with an expression that she couldn't read, and Sky turned and headed back inside.

Eva, not waiting for Sky or anyone else to return, turned and left.

Chapter Fifteen

"Wakey, wake!" Chas's voice sounded louder than it needed to be.

Sky groaned and reached for her head, pain pounding everywhere.

"Damn it. How much did I drink?" She blinked slowly and noticed she was lying on Chas's couch.

"Too much. Maxine and James are on their way with mimosas," he said cheerfully.

"How are you even up?" Sky questioned. She didn't know what time it was, but she knew it was too early.

"Hell… when I go into the city, us gay men can stay up till eight in the morning and be at work by noon." Chas walked away and returned with orange juice and water. "Reboot and get your ass up."

"I don't even have clothes to change into," Sky complained. "Slow down."

Chas laughed. "Maxine stopped by your dad's and has fresh stuff for you. We have a lot to talk about!"

Sky frowned. "Like what?" she whined.

Chas lips pursed and he smirked.

"We don't know but we are going to find out."

In another ten minutes, Maxine and James arrived, handed Sky a bag and pointed toward the bathroom. Sky took the opportunity to shower, purposely at a slow pace, to sort through the night. The last thing she remembered was… her thoughts drew blank, and she grimaced, unable to concentrate.

"Damn it."

Eventually, she had to come out and when she did, the smell of pancakes and bacon flooded her nose. She walked lazily into the dining room; her friends were making her a plate.

"Sit. Eat," Chas ordered.

"I called your dad and told him you were in recovery mode," Maxine said. "I know you originally planned to go visit him this morning, but that ship has sailed."

Sky gave a half wave and grumbled as she took a bite. They ate for a bit until Sky noticed Chas sneaking looks at Maxine.

"What?"

Maxine looked up with concern.

"Do you remember last night?" She clearly was stalling to ask what she really wanted to know.

Irritated, Sky crossed her arms.

"Can y'all just spit it out already?"

"I told you tiptoeing wouldn't work," Chas said. He looked at Sky and smiled. "Last night. Right after the New Year arrived. You walked into the bar, alone might we all add and highly emotional."

Sky stared, that memory not forming in her head. She frowned.

"What was I doing outside?"

Maxine answered. "You were out there with Eva. I'd come to tell y'all to come back inside but at the end, only you returned."

What was she supposed to say to that? Sky shrugged.

"I don't know. Why were we outside?"

"Eva was outside. You went to go find her and you did." Maxine looked like she wanted to shake some memory back into Sky and added, "And when you came back, you had tears in your eyes."

"I did?" Sky couldn't think of what could have occurred that night. Even when she got drunk in the past, she always remembered everything that happened. Part of her was afraid to remember now but she knew she had to. Because, if anyone remembered it was Eva and she owed it to her not to forget. Clearly something had happened.

"Yes. The last time you cried like that was when your mom died," Maxine said softly. "It was as if you lost someone all over again."

Sky's frown deepened. That was a strong statement to make but one she knew Maxine wouldn't make lightly. She took a drink of water and shut her eyes. A memory of Boyd flashed in her mind.

"I saw Boyd and some of his old friends. I think one of them was harassing her." Sky looked up. "Maybe that was it."

"They weren't there when I peeked out," Maxine stated.

Sky continued to think about it, and she almost gave up when she pictured Eva's sad eyes and distant stare. Then all at once, her memories came flooding back to her; Sky found her eyes widening as she covered her mouth with her hand. Stunned by her own careless actions, Sky groaned and hissed out profanity. Everyone stared in anticipation and all Sky could do was look up and shake her head, ready to cry.

"She's never going to talk to me again," she hissed. "Fuck. I'm so stupid. What was I thinking?"

"What are you talking about?" Chas reached across the table, hand pressed into hers, doing his best to comfort Sky even though she didn't deserve it.

"Whatever it is… it can't be that bad. I can tell… Eva adores you." Maxine tried to cheer her up.

Sky looked at her friends and told them.

"I kissed her!" she said in a whisper.

Maxine, James, and Chas all looked to be taking her confession well, no surprise in their calm demeanor. Sky thought for a second that they hadn't heard her.

"I said, I kissed her."

Maxine nodded. "We heard you."

"Then…" Sky was about to freak out. She had expected a more dramatic response than what she was getting., "Can y'all act a little surprised by this because…" she pointed to herself… "I am."

"But we're not," Chas said, directly looking into Sky's eyes. "You've been obvious on our end. She does something for you and maybe because she's not someone you'd expect to go for, you've been in denial but… it's…" Chas closed his mouth and ended it there, leaving Sky on the edge of her seat.

"It's what?" Sky shook her head. "No. Eva's… sweet and even funny in her Eva way. But…" Sky didn't know what to say next.

"But what?" Maxine questioned, annoyed. "Are you really acting this shallow, or do you just not see it?"

Sky opened and then closed her mouth. She didn't know what to say to that. She stood and needed to leave. There was only one person who could help her through this, and she needed clarity now.

"I'm not trying to make you feel bad," Maxine said sincerely. "We just—"

Sky waved her hand out and cut her friend off.

"I'm sorry. It's not you guys. You see things the way you do, and I acknowledge you care for her. I need to go see my dad."

"Then I'll take you," Maxine offered.

"No. I need to be alone for a minute. I'm getting an Uber now. He always helps me think," Sky admitted.

Maxine looked at her friend, honestly relieved that she was going to her father. If one thing was certain, he'd help Sky to realize what she needed to.

Sky walked back to them, and they each embraced her. After a few minutes, her Uber had arrived and she said her goodbyes and left, needing her dad to find a way to fix her mistakes.

*

The second Sky walked into the room and saw her dad sitting up tall in the bed, looking healthier than ever, she let the tears fall. Her dad's smile vanished, concern for his daughter running through his mind.

"What's wrong with my little girl?" She knelt and he embraced Sky tightly as she sobbed in his arms.

Sky couldn't say the words, afraid he would be mad at her. He adored Eva and considered her just as much of a daughter.

"Dad... I screwed up and I don't know what to do."

"Okay," he cooed and let her sob for as long as she needed. "Nothing sad lasts forever, honey. Whatever it may be, I know you will do the right thing to make things better."

It took Sky a few minutes to collect herself and she straightened to face him.

"Talk to me," he encouraged.

She wiped her eyes and looked at her dad as if he were a lifeline that kept her afloat.

"I…" she sighed. "There's no excuse for what I did. I was drunk but… I didn't have to do what I did."

He squeezed her hand, no judgment in his eyes.

"Does this involve Eva?" he asked, softly.

She sank her fingers into her forehead and nodded.

"We were out. I think she got into it with one of the guys back from high school. She was ready to leave after that and I tried to convince her to stay." Sky frowned, replaying the memory in her head as she sighed. "I don't know what pushed me to react so… irresponsibly and inappropriate… but without warning, I kissed her. You know that's not like me to act without thinking, Dad, but that's what I did. I didn't think."

Sky had to fight not to cry. "She was so mad, Dad."

He nodded and opened his arms for her to fall back into.

"It's going to be okay."

Sky couldn't believe that. All she could remember was anger and hurt, followed by Eva's stern words. Maxine was right about her trifling toward Eva. There was no question that Sky respected Eva as a person, but since the beginning she had never considered Eva an option to be with in an intimate way. Eva didn't fit the kind of woman she wanted and therefore, she was automatically disqualified.

"You know how much she's struggled to open up. I feel like all I've been doing is asking her to give more and then when she finally does, I go and do this."

"Sit down." He pointed to the sofa chair beside him, and she moved to sit. He gave her a thoughtful look before stating his opinion. "What you did was not the right move, but Eva is stronger than she looks. What concerns me is what your plan is after this?"

Sky stared, completely at a loss for words.

"I need to go talk to her."

"And what will you say? Why did you kiss her? She deserves to know why."

That made Sky reconsider reaching out to Eva; she wanted to hide.

"Damn." She wanted to do the right thing, but she didn't have an answer.

"Why are you working so hard to not let yourself feel what you're experiencing?" Her dad was baffled by how closed off she was to not be able to see what was obviously transpiring. It was either that, or Sky wanted to pretend she had no feelings for Eva. "I'm not asking because I want to challenge your feelings. I seriously want to know."

Sky sometimes found it hard to express her feelings or sit in those thoughts when they scared her, so she normally acknowledged them from a distance until they were forgotten. Her relationships in the last three years had been different from her previous experiences. Sky no longer gravitated toward the women she used to go for and was now seeking out someone with more of a home comfort feeling. But as her dad questioned her about why she was so closed off, Sky knew the answer.

"I watched you and mom through so many stages of your life together. The good and bad. I got to see how it was to really love someone and the teamwork you two shared. No one could get in between the two of you. Not even your kids." Sky smiled. "When we lost Mom, it shattered me and gave me a hard slap to the face." She looked off to the side at no particular thing and sighed. "I'd been dating for all the right reasons, but I also was dating with all the wrong expectations in who my person should be. Does that make sense?" She frowned.

Her dad nodded and reached to hold her hand.

Sky licked her dry lips and smiled faintly at him before she continued.

"I had to start from scratch, and I honestly haven't been dating much but deep down, I knew enough that I wanted the kind of love you and Mom had. The kind that felt warm, affectionate, together." Sky groaned and wiped her tears away as quickly as they fell. She looked down at her fingers laced into her dad's. "I think I'm afraid of love. I saw how losing Mom affected you. But more than that… I'm afraid I'd never be enough, and also too much, for someone like the kind of woman I'd need."

"Oh, honey. I have never thought of you as too much and any woman or human who thinks that needs their head examined."

Sky smiled. "Thanks Dad."

"Now, I'm going to ask you a very big question and you don't have to answer me, but I will encourage you to answer it for yourself." Her dad's cryptic encouragement made Sky's heart rate pick up.

She nodded slowly.

He smiled.

"Do you think that you might care about Eva a bit more than you've been admitting to yourself?"

Sky seemed taken aback by his question even though she should have expected it. What was it about Eva that kept Sky thinking about her? She'd been making up several different reasons for wanting to be near Eva a lot lately but none of her reasons could stick.

"She reminds me of Mom." Sky laughed, hearing how that sounded. "Obviously, she's not Mom but she holds similar qualities and tasteful lifestyle choices that Mom had and in some… unexpected way, Eva began to feel like home."

Her dad's smile was wide.

"That's what pulled me to speak to her at the bar. I'd walk in and she'd be tucked in a corner, drawing on a sketch pad, wearing her sweaters and whispering the same classic tunes your mom listened to. She helped me heal. And getting to know her… Eva is just an amazing woman who is so loving but so hidden. Like a pearl in the sea."

Sky nodded. "Yeah. I don't think I've ever gotten over Mom. Being near Eva has been so healing."

He nodded. "But she's not Mom."

Sky snorted. "Oh, I know!"

He squinted his eyes playfully.

"You still haven't answered my question."

Sky groaned, wishing he'd forgotten and leaned back into the chair.

"I honestly don't know, Dad. I think… I'm confused."

He nodded. "That's fair." He looked focused before saying, "I think what you need to do is start acknowledging how important she is to you. And don't try to hide from your feelings and instead, lean into them and challenge yourself."

"And lastly," Sky said knowingly.

"And lastly…" He grinned. "Tell her what you want out of the connection you have so far and make sure she knows how much you mean that."

Sky took in her dad's guidance, nodding slowly. "I can do that."

"Good. No time like the present," he encouraged.

There was still so much time left in the day and Sky had no clue where Eva was, but she was sure she wasn't at Maxine's coffee shop. Her only other option would be Eva's home. Could she just show up, uninvited? She could at least try and text, hoping Eva agreed to meet.

Chapter Sixteen

"Sabrina couldn't make it." Denise held up two smoothies and walked inside.

It was freezing outside, Eva moved promptly to shut the door. It was snowing, not too much, but enough for Eva to make plans later to clear off her porch and pathway before it turned to ice tonight.

They walked into the living room. Denise sat on the floor next to the fireplace, trying to stay warm.

Eva sat on the ottoman she kept on the side of the couch, and Denise handed her the peanut butter and banana smoothie.

"Why did you buy me this? I could have made it myself."

Denise rolled her eyes and tucked her knees in, arms curled around them. She always found Eva's nit-picky behavior adorable and sometimes did things on purpose just to hear her complain.

"Yes, you could have made it, but you didn't. So, I bought you one."

"I entertain you, don't I?" Eva asked, squinting her eyes at Denise in accusation.

Denise smiled coyly.

Eva sniffed the shake before tasting it. The peanut butter overpowered the shake exactly how she liked it and Eva smiled.

"See. I knew you'd like it. Don't be so difficult." Denise began to drink her shake before it lost its texture and thickness. She watched Eva consume hers, occasionally looking away, trying not to seem so invasive.

Eva could feel Denise's gaze and sighed.

"What?"

Denise snorted and straightened.

"I was supposed to do this with Sabrina, but she did leave me her footnotes."

Eva decided to face the music Denise was about to sing.

"Let's get this over with."

"It's been two days, and we haven't seen you since you disappeared New Year's Eve." Denise dramatized her voice, as if she were a moderator in a political debate. "Our first question is, what is the main reason you left that night?"

Eva sighed. "It was too much, too soon. It felt as if I'd been in a cave only to step into the sunlight without protection after months of darkness."

"And?" Denise pushed.

There was no point in hiding the truth. Eventually, Denise and Sabrina would find out. If she didn't tell them, and they found out from Maxine or anyone closely related to that inner circle, she'd never have heard the end of it.

"She kissed me." Eva had to practically shout the words out. Partially because she wasn't ready to talk about it, but she was also concerned with how Denise might react. Eva snuck a swift glance at Denise, noticing a look of contemplation streaked across her face. "It was random and something I didn't expect, to be honest." Eva thought she needed to explain more but it only deepened Denise's expression.

"Did you like it?" Denise asked in what sounded like a small voice.

That was not the response Eva wanted to hear. She looked dubious and placed her shake on the coffee table. "It was unexpected." She hadn't processed any feelings regarding being kissed by Sky and had no intention of doing so.

If there was one thing Eva liked to be, it was realistic and consistent in living that way. If she pictured anything between her and Sky at this point, it was merely as acquaintances.

Denise struggled to believe that.

"There is no right or wrong answer. Only your truth."

Eva wanted to be honest, but she wasn't naïve. Their relationship had ended prematurely because of Eva's private lifestyle.

"If I'm being honest, I'm trying not to think about it. She was drunk and I'd just dealt with an idiot I try to avoid on the regular."

Denise shifted her body and stared into the fire as she spoke.

"Even after almost two years, I still cling onto the hope of having something real with you."

"That's…" Eva knew it would take someone very patient to truly understand her and she had no doubt Denise understood her. But was that enough to say she could build a life with her and live their mutual authentic selves?

"I know. Sky's the first woman to pull you out of hiding and that says it all." Denise spoke softly but her voice cracked; it was hard to accept that she'd never get her chance with Eva and that she had to move on. "You don't have to see it right now. Your walls are very tall at the moment. But…" she narrowed her eyes. "But if you want to have your ultimate dreams come true, you can't stay hidden, not even with yourself." Denise let out a dramatic groan and straightened.

"Now that we've gotten that out into the open…" Denise's brows perked, eager to ask more questions. "I know you're probably questioning why you got entangled in Sky's web, but you did say you'd help with the school theater program. Are you still going to?"

Eva had given her word that she'd assist and to break that now would ruin her own integrity, which Eva had no intentions of doing. She'd gotten several texts and two missed calls from Sky since that night and Eva hadn't built up the courage to respond. She knew she had to answer if she'd still show up for the theater program. Chas had already sent her an email with everything she'd need to know to assist with editing and the concept of what he envisioned for the portraits and portfolio of the entire production.

"I said I would," was all Eva could say.

It was Monday and until now, Eva had kept the idea of facing Sky in the back of her mind.

"This is good for you." Denise leaned forward and squeezed Eva's arm. "Leave Sky out and consider what this exposure could do for your career and position in this town. It's long overdue for you to end the title of *mysterious loner nerd*."

Eva grumbled, "Is that what everyone calls me?"

"More or less." Denise shrugged. "My point is the perk to living in a diverse, yet small town, is that there's room for growth and most people here want to see healthy change. You could bring so much to this town."

"I'm a designer and artist. How?" Eva asked sarcastically.

Denise laughed. "Well for starters, because you work in the tech world, you are a problem solver for businesses and can help them attract consumers from an online platform. Have you seen our town website and other local businesses? You could teach tech and your artistry could liven up this town. Don't play me with all those lame ass excuses as to why you're better hidden."

Eva grinned. "Fine. I got the message. Don't go backwards just because of a hiccup."

"Yeah." Denise shrugged. "Something like that." Denise stood. "All right. My job here is done. I'll let you get back to whatever it was you were doing."

They walked to the door together in silence. When Denise opened it, she turned and reached in and cupped Eva's cheek.

"I'm happy that you're finally allowing people to see you." She leaned in and kissed Eva's cheek before turning away and leaving.

Chapter Seventeen

"Hey. Everyone, listen up." Chas waved his arms out, signaling for his students to quiet down.

The classroom was twice the size of a normal room, with a centered stage where normally a teacher's desk would be. Instead, Chas's desk was tucked in the corner next to a window. About three dozen chairs were placed in a wide circle where they all sat, waiting for Chas to speak.

Sky sat between a few students before they separated into smaller groups to rehearse the parts they'd been given. There were an equal number of boys and girls, all between the ages of fourteen to seventeen, eager to learn their lines.

"Now that you have all received your lines, it's important for each of you to think about the kind of character you want to resemble, that reflects your own personality. Since we have an actual cosmetic artist who can make you look like the version of the character you want to see reflected, think long and hard," Chas encouraged. He was great with teens, and they seemed to really listen to what he had to say.

"Anything to add, Ms. Wyman?" Chas asked, giving Sky the opportunity to speak.

She wasn't used to being called by her last name. She smiled and spoke confidently.

"As soon as you have a picture in your head of what you'd want your character to look like, I'll sketch it and get your approvals before I begin working!"

"This is so freaking cool," a fifteen-year-old non-binary teen cast as Dracula, said excitedly.

Other students agreed and began talking amongst themselves, eager to begin learning their lines.

"Don't forget." Chas's brows raised to enhance his dramatic high-pitched voice and they all turned his way, a few snickering. "We will begin stage rehearsals next week. I need you all to be comfortable with your lines. I'm not expecting you to remember them word for word just yet, but at least have a comfortable tone to your voice when we begin. Catch my meaning?" he asked.

"It's caught," all his students said in unison.

"Okay. You can begin practicing and I'll have one last surprise for you before we leave." Chas stood and the students began splitting off into smaller groups.

Sky stood and followed him to his desk. She grabbed a chair and took a seat. She crossed her legs and arms over her chest and looked at Chas, drinking his bottled water with his eyes shut.

"What's this surprise you have for the kids?" she asked.

Chas drank a few more gulps and put the bottle on the table.

"You'll see." He wiggled his brows, being coy.

"You know I hate surprises, right?" Sky reminded him.

"No!" Chas narrowed his eyes and grinned. "You hate not being in the know of it all."

Sky shook her head. "That's the same thing," she replied.

Chas rolled his eyes and dug through one of the cabinets in his desk drawer to grab his laptop.

"What I need to do is go over an estimate of how much all of this will cost to make sure I don't go too over the budget the school gave us."

"Are you concerned about not having enough to cover everything?" Sky knew Chas didn't do halfway and that meant he'd want the play and his students to look their very best.

He sighed, rested his elbow on the table and whispered.

"This is only my third year running the program and the first year, the school could only afford my salary. We didn't even charge anyone to come watch the kids perform until the last performance when we finally had a more than just the parents come watch."

"What about last year?" Sky asked.

"We charged for every play, and more people came but the budget was tight. I used a lot of my own money, and the school created a small budget. But this year has started off rocky. I need this next play to show the school and the town that it's worth keeping."

Sky could see the worry in Chas's eyes and didn't like it.

"If it helps, I can go back to the city and grab my personal kit."

"You are already helping me for free. I don't want you to use your own supplies," Chas said.

Sky shook her head. "I can and I will."

He smiled and she knew she'd made the right call.

The door to the classroom opened and to Sky's surprise, she looked up to find Eva standing in the doorway.

Sky's heart skipped, watching Eva walk into the classroom with her backpack draped at her side. She hadn't mentally prepared for what to say but she hoped Eva would give her another chance.

Palms suddenly sweaty, Sky stood, brushing her hands over her jeans. She took a long breath and released it. Her mouth shut, and lips sealed tightly, Sky gave a half smile.

Eva couldn't make eye contact with her, and Sky dropped her gaze feeling defeated.

"Hey." Eva stood awkwardly; hands hidden in her pants pockets.

"Thanks for making it," Chas said, offering a sincere smile. They shook hands and Sky tried not to take it personally when Eva only nodded at her. "Please, grab a chair," Chas offered.

Eva walked away for a brief moment and placed a chair next to Sky and sat quietly. She slid her backpack off and placed it beside her chair.

Occasionally, Sky snuck glances at Eva, who was doing a good job of avoiding her. Sky sighed, aware that now was not the time to try and talk.

"You came in at the perfect time. Right now, they have all received their lines and are focused on reading the story itself and getting an idea of how their characters would be." Chas spoke in a professional manner as he updated Eva on what she'd missed. "Today, I just wanted you to see the students and get a good sense of how we do things. I'm hoping by tomorrow, you can start sketching."

"To be clear, the concept for the art portfolio is to tell a story directly through drawings. More specifically, a story that shows this theater production's journey?" Eva questioned. "And with the videos… do you want it to be more like a movie of their journey and potentially useful for their submissions to whatever future path they take?"

"Exactly," Chas admitted. "I plan to turn all the drawings and photography from both of your artistry into a book to be sold."

He looked at both of them and sighed.

"I am very thankful that you have come to help us. I know it was a big ask. The only thing I really hope you'll say yes to, is for the both of you to build the portfolio book together."

Sky shifted in her seat and noticed Eva frown. Was what she did so bad that Eva never wanted to be alone with her ever again? Sky wouldn't pressure her, so she sat in silence and waited for Eva to make her choice.

It took Eva only a few seconds to decide.

"I suppose that wouldn't be too much of an inconvenience."

Sky frowned but accepted the win. She believed if given the chance, she could break through one of Eva's walls and get her to listen.

"Thanks." Chas smiled. "Feel free to observe and if you have any questions, I'll be right here trying to crunch some numbers."

Eva nodded and stood, moving the chair to the opposite end where she could sit alone. Sky watched her pull a sketch pad and pencil from her backpack and look around in the direction of the kids.

"Give her space," Chas said quietly.

Sky groaned but nodded. Instead of walking over to Eva, she decided to go to a small group of girls, sitting huddled in a corner on the floor. If she distracted herself long enough, being ignored by Eva wouldn't hurt so much.

Chapter Eighteen

Over the next three days, Eva went to the high school and sketched what she felt were memorable moments between the students and Chas. And every time, Sky seemed to be included, as she often sat with the teens.

It was Thursday and she planned on leaving as soon as she was finished with the sketch she was currently working on. It was of two teen boys whose roles were two individuals with significant physical strength. The girl who'd be playing Mina had been nervous to be picked up, so Sky had agreed to be the test dummy and allow the boys to pick her up.

Both boys lifted the chair high with Sky sitting in it. Sky looked comfortable and unafraid as they walked and sat her down on the other side of the room.

All the students laughed and cheered, the girl ultimately being confident in the boys' abilities.

"You never talk. Is that on purpose?" Eva was caught off guard by a teen hunched over her shoulder. "My name's Chasity. They, them pronouns."

Eva smiled politely at them.

"I'm not much of a talker," Eva admitted. "At least, not in the beginning." She offered her hand. "I'm Eva."

"Your drawing is freaking insane," they admired. Chasity sat in the chair beside Eva and tapped their feet three times and then stopped, doing it again a couple seconds later. "Are you the one who will be drawing each of us individually? And what are your pronouns?"

Eva smiled, dropping her pencil on the sketch pad.

"Yes, I'll be drawing everyone here and my pronouns are she, her."

"That's cool." Chasity continued to tap their feet. "But who will draw you?"

Eva never considered being a part of the portfolio. She considered herself merely an outside aide with no ties to the program.

"I am here only to draw and help out with editing all the film."

"You're good with computers too?" they asked enthusiastically, feet still tapping in sets of threes.

Eva nodded. "I'm a software engineer, product, graphic, and gaming designer."

Chasity's eyes widened and smiled big as they snapped their fingers as if it helped to release some of their overstimulated excitement.

"No way! I watch a lot of YouTube videos on tech creations. I want to become an animator and game designer."

"Really?" Eva responded in shock. Denise had been right. Living in a small town, finding tech programs wasn't easy to come by. "I have a personalized AI that teaches individuals effective ways to make the tech world work for you. It's through my Instagram."

Eva provided Chasity with her Instagram just as Sky walked up.

"Hey, Chas wants to have a quick word with everyone. You should get to it." Sky smiled and watched Chasity leave. She'd been giving Eva space and it had taken everything in her not to push before Eva was ready.

"You can sit, if you'd like." Eva surprised herself with that offer.

Sky's brows arched, surprised too. She wouldn't second guess Eva or squander an opportunity to share space with her, so she sat.

"Thanks."

Eva tilted her head and opened her sketchbook back to finish the outline of her drawing, going off memory. She had a work meeting later today and wanted a few hours of quiet, so she needed to get finished here. She drew the structure of the room from the angle of where she'd watched the boys picking up Sky several minutes prior, focused on getting the angular proportions right.

"Did you invite me to sit here... because you are being nice... or?" Sky whispered low so that only Eva could hear.

Chas was talking to the students, and they were on the other side of the room so as not to disrupt them.

Eva stopped what she was doing and tilted her head to give Sky a considerable lengthy gaze. There was still anger present in the pit of her belly, but Eva didn't want that to show. She'd weighed all the reasons why Sky would kiss her and not once did the thought of Sky doing it as a joke or to toy with her come to mind. That left very few options but one that still meant Sky had been careless and rash. But that didn't mean Sky had any unkind intent.

"Can't I invite you to sit down simply because it's not good to have this negative energy around them?" Eva looked toward the students attentively listening to Chas as he gave them the plans for the next few weeks.

Sky's expression skewed, observing the students while digesting Eva's words. After a moment, her eyebrows knitted together, and she sighed.

"Is that the only reason?"

"Why can't you let things be without you knowing the reasons behind it?" Eva was asking out of curiosity more than frustration.

Sky had never been asked that question in a serious manner before. People complained or asked hypothetically but, never in a way to really understand Sky's reasons for being overtly inquisitive. Lips pressed into a tight line, Sky thought about it. She wanted to give an honest answer.

"I suppose, I got it from my mom. Growing up, my siblings and I would call her *detective momma.*" Sky laughed lightly and earned a few looks from the students. She waved apologetically and waited for their attention to be back on Chas before speaking again in a quieter tone. "She'd tell us to never judge someone for their choices if you didn't know the why behind it. When my brother punched a kid one year and got suspended from school, she could have just grounded him. But she asked why. The teachers didn't even ask that."

Eva tilted her head in curiosity.

"Why did he punch the kid?"

Sky smiled. "Because my brother picked up my younger sister after she finished volleyball practice every day and that boy had cornered my sister in the girl's locker room. My brother heard her scream, ran right in, and punched the boy. The boy ran out and told a teacher, nose busted and they just… suspended my brother."

Eva frowned and nodded.

"Her inquisitive genes rubbed off on me, I guess." Sky shrugged. "There are other reasons why I tend to want to know something, and sometimes it is as simple as wanting to be in the know of things. But for you… maybe I ask so many questions… because I want to know everything about you. How you think and why? What makes you smile?" Sky averted her eyes awkwardly as if she'd been confessing to something deeper than surface level curiosity. Perhaps, she was.

"Stuff like that." Feeling vulnerable, Sky straightened in her seat and crossed her legs.

Eva nodded. She could understand Sky a bit more and she didn't want to neglect that new knowledge.

"I wanted you to sit beside me, because… I miss getting to know you." She let out a shaky breath.

Sky smiled; her hope being restored.

"I miss you too."

So much of the tension between them dissolved with each breath they took. They looked up at the same time as the students stood, dismissed from their meeting. They were grabbing their belongings, heading out as they waved goodbyes.

Chas walked up, head shaking, with a wide grin on his face.

"I see you two have made up. Finally."

Sky snorted. "Thanks for pointing out the obvious."

He smirked. "Anytime." He looked at the sketch Eva had exposed for them to see. "How's it coming along?"

"I have no doubt that you'll love it. I also have a few ideas that I plan to do with the drawings." Eva didn't elaborate, choosing at that moment to put her sketchbook away. "I should get going. I have work to finish."

Eva stood and contemplated saying anything more. They had admitted to missing connecting, but it still hadn't changed the elephant in the room. She didn't know how to bring it up and wouldn't in front of Chas's watchful gaze.

To Eva's relief, Sky spoke up first.

"Perhaps we can go over some ideas for the portfolio over dinner at my dad's place."

Eva's head lifted, surprised by the offer and how nervous Sky had sounded.

"Uh…" She smiled awkwardly but nodded. "Send me the details and I'll be there."

"Okay." Sky agreed.

Eva nodded and left with only a wave as a goodbye.

Chapter Nineteen

Sky had not wasted any time in seeing Eva again. When Eva knocked on the front door of her dad's house the next evening, it was a relief to know they'd have all the time they needed to work through some things.

"Thanks for dinner. It was amazing." Eva stood, signaling she was ready to leave.

Sky reached for their empty glasses to take into the kitchen, but Eva moved to grab them first.

"The least I can do is clean," Eva offered.

Sky smiled. "You know damn well I didn't make dinner."

"Maybe not, but you provided." Eva held the two glasses up. "I can do the dishes."

Sky waved for her to continue helping and they walked into the kitchen together, Eva reaching the sink. It wouldn't take her long since there were only a few dishes, so Sky leaned back into the counter to watch.

After much internal deliberation, Sky had made up her mind on how to address the kiss and knew they couldn't go past tonight without discussing it. She only hoped Eva was on board with talking about it, or at least listening.

Sky waited patiently, replaying the words she needed to say in her head, stroking her cheek in deep thought, unaware that Eva was finished. When she snapped out of her thoughts, Sky found Eva standing a foot away, wryly.

Sky sucked in a lot of air and released it loudly.

"I swear, I usually don't get this nervous."

Eva squinted her eyes, finding Sky's honesty refreshing in an unexpected way.

"I suppose you aren't usually someone who kisses a person you're not into."

How was Sky supposed to respond to that? She thought Eva was amazing and one of the most creative and insightful women she'd ever met. It had been a long time since she admired someone so profoundly. But attracted, Sky couldn't say that. Couldn't because she wasn't ready to or didn't want to, she didn't know. Or maybe, she just wasn't at all. Despite her inner conflict, it felt wrong admitting to something she wasn't sure about.

To deflect, Sky smiled.

"I'm not used to acting impulsive and without consideration for the person who could be affected by my choices."

Eva seemed content with that response.

"I know I should give you some level of grace. You were intoxicated after all."

"Me being drunk is no excuse and I'd say you've given me plenty of grace." Eva looked doubtful and Sky continued. "You took a risk in opening up to me. Someone who never noticed you before that day when you caught me. And even after, I'd been making you uncomfortable and then when we finally start building a friendship, I do something reckless." Sky waved her hands between them. "And here you are now, giving me another opportunity."

"You've helped me too," Eva said, in the most tender and soft voice.

Sky frowned. "By making your life louder, as of late." She huffed out a laugh. "Doubtful."

"You saved my life," Eva rushed out breathlessly. Her jaw tightened, not having intended to say that aloud. Eva never planned to tell Sky the truth but here she was now, bringing it up.

Sky looked even more confused.

Eva frowned and shook her head.

"Never mind. Forget what I said." She moved to leave.

"Wait!" Sky shouted as Eva walked past her toward the front door. She didn't want to force her to stay but she wanted to understand and know when she left, they would be okay. "Please!" Sky pleaded.

Eva was halfway through the living room when she stopped. She shut her eyes and tilted her head up, not sure if she was ready to reveal a secret that she'd kept to herself all these years.

"Can you just... sit with me? Please," Sky asked softly. She had grown to care so much for Eva in a short time, and she couldn't stand the sight of seeing Eva in pain.

Eva turned, scared, but she knew if they were ever going to become real friends, Sky deserved to know. So, she followed Sky to the couch and sat.

Sky didn't hesitate to reach in and link their fingers. "Please, tell me what you meant?"

Eva couldn't remember the last time her heart felt so heavy and filled with so much sorrow. It was almost too hard to breathe. It was hard not to miss the compassion and support in Sky's brown eyes.

"That night. When some of our classmates thought it would be funny to print out copies of my personal queer-based art and write the things they did on it and present it at prom. Let's just say, I was done. It's one thing to call me names and mock me. But to take something precious that I loved, personal to me, and humiliate me with it, calling out an auction for anyone who wanted to give a poor orphan loner dyke a chance at love." Eva shook her head. "I felt broken that night. My group home was counting the days until I turned eighteen. The scholarship I'd hoped for fell through and I thought I wasn't going to be able to afford college. Then to be outed through my own art..."

Sky listened, very aware of the tears in her own eyes. She hadn't known anything about Eva back then, other than her being in foster care. And to even think of how she used to address her, even in her own head, Sky was disgusted with the teenage version of herself. She'd been taught better.

"I only went to prom because I thought it was better than sitting around in the group home. I figured I'd sit in a corner and draw, getting free food in the process," Eva admitted. She sighed and looked up. "But after what they did, all I could think about was ending my own misery. So, I ran off towards the trail I often hiked alone. The one I took you to."

"It would have taken you two hours to get there by foot," Sky said.

Eva nodded. "It would have but I would have walked every step to get there if you hadn't chased after me."

Sky watched as Eva struggled to continue. She squeezed her hand and spoke in a gentle voice. "Why were you headed there?"

Eva's smile didn't reach her eyes.

"To end it all." She sounded so matter of fact and serious.

There was no misunderstanding what Eva meant by that. The idea of Eva not being here right now to sit beside her made the tears fall from Sky's eyes. She wiped them away, feeling wrong for crying.

"I'm sorry. This is your journey. I just... never expected to hear that."

Eva nodded. "It was our journey. You just never knew it. I never thought I'd tell anyone this... let alone you." Eva laughed, seeing the irony in it all. There was an unexpected sense of relief in telling Sky everything. She thought about her dad and sighed. "It would have broken his heart for me to take a place that was shared in love and happy memories, only to darken it. It was hard losing him and being left alone, surrounded by people who didn't understand me."

"I'm glad you didn't hurt yourself." Sky reached in to link their fingers.

"I am too," Eva admitted. "I watched my dad fight so hard to live. He made me promise to always fight for life and I almost failed him." Eva looked up, smiling weakly. "He had stage four prostate cancer. I was there the day he passed. He looked at me and said, 'I'm still living because of you, baby.' That was the last thing he said."

Sky brushed the tears from Eva's face, cupping her cheek as she continued to listen.

"Those words you said to me the night of prom reminded me of the promises I'd made to my dad. I have never forgotten them. It's what turned me around and pushed me to believe there had to be more to life than what I knew at the time."

Sky had chased after her, unable to see the sadness that was in Eva's eyes the night of prom. She never knew her words would be held in such significance.

"I'm sorry for it all. And I know you don't blame me for anything, but I could have done more. Told my parents. Someone else. I know my mom would have stormed into that school and cursed everyone out. She probably would have adopted you right then and there. And it's clear my dad should have adopted you."

Eva laughed. "Things worked out at the end for me." She held Sky's gaze for the longest time. "I appreciate you saying that." She sighed. "When it came down to the finish line, you were there for me."

"When I said those words to you, I have to admit, I needed to hear them for myself too," Sky said, drawing Eva's attention. "I was very closeted until college. And in some selfish way, I thought if you could make it through that night, I could make it through mine when the time came. I found you bold and defiant to the mundane, even back then. That's why you stood out to so many classmates. Unfortunately, back then, and even now, being different brings on the potential for being judged."

"Intensity intensifies body's strength and mind's growth," Eva whispered. She smiled. "Those were the first words you said to me, right before you gave me the biggest speech."

"And I was right. You turned out to be one of the most successful people in our town, let alone our graduating class and even the most popular girls who never noticed you before desire you." Sky grinned.

Eva snorted through her laughter and Sky's eyes widened in surprise, laughing too.

"I thought you were so full of shit when you said, *one day, all the girls will want you.*" Eva rolled her eyes. "I mean… I have dated, I guess, but I wouldn't say the most popular girls have really wanted me."

"Oh really?" Sky narrowed her eyes in a challenge. "Other than Denise, who isn't from here but has an amazing personality and is gorgeous as fuck, you dated Maxine, the star of track and field and ex-cheerleader. And there has to be a few more women we don't know about."

Eva's lips seemed to seal as she hid a smile.

"See!" Sky acknowledged.

"I wouldn't say Maxine and I *dated* dated. There was never an open date involved." Eva was awkward in saying that, but it was the truth.

"Maybe not, but there were real feelings between the two of you."

Eva nodded. "Yeah. There were. I guess your words did hold truer than I allowed them to. But I think I've reached all I'll reach to finding someone special, unique, and of the popular variety," Eva joked.

"That's not true," Sky whispered.

Their gazes met and Sky forgot how their conversation had drifted there. Sky's chest felt as if it were about to explode with emotion, the sound of her pulse pounding with vivid images of kissing Eva parading across her mind, and it all made sense now. Her unknown questions were being answered in this very instant.

Sky shut her eyes before she did anything impulsive again.

"Oh my god!"

"What?" Eva asked quietly, very much aware that Sky's behavior had suddenly changed.

"Huh?" Sky looked up. *Damn.*

She had not intended to say anything aloud.

"Oh, uh…" Sky swallowed. "I… umm… forgot, that…" She needed to come up with something to recover from her awkward change. She pushed on both temples, trying to limit her racing thoughts and eyebrows suddenly drooped in fatigue. "I was supposed to bring Dad leftovers tonight," she ended up saying.

That was actually true, but it wasn't that big of a deal.

"Oh," Eva frowned, not sure if that was the full truth but she wouldn't question her about it. "Okay. I should head out anyway." Eva stood. "Thanks again for dinner and listening. I'm glad we talked."

Sky nodded, following her to the door.

"I'm happy we did too." She opened it and Eva stepped onto the porch. Before she disappeared into the night, Sky called out. "Are we good? I know—"

Eva held her hand up before Sky could say more.

"We're moving forward."

"Okay!" Sky nodded. "Night."

Eva waved goodbye and Sky watched her leave, knowing she was in trouble.

*

"You do acknowledge that I have a healthy reputation to uphold," Sky's father questioned. "You coming in here after hours and begging the nurses to let you into my room could add me to the watch list."

Sky had driven to the rehabilitation facility several minutes after Eva had left, in need of her dad's advice. It was after nine and visiting hours had ended an hour ago.

With a little convincing, making it appear as if it was an emergency, Sky had been granted twenty minutes.

"Please, Dad. This is serious, and they'll be back to retrieve me before you know it." Sky was not in a joking mood.

Her dad's brows perked.

"And is this so serious you couldn't wait till morning?"

Sky knew the answer to that.

"Does it matter now?" She ignored the question.

He grumbled but waved his hand for her to share what she came here to say.

"Go on, my child!"

"I'm…" Suddenly Sky was afraid to say the words aloud. She never thought she'd utter words like this so quickly. But it was her truth, and she needed some guidance. She was also surprised within herself.

He frowned. "This is serious." He pressed the button on the bed remote to position him further upright. "Tell me," he encouraged.

"I'm falling… I'm…" Was she really about to admit something so big and significant? Sky was afraid to make it real.

"Honey. You're torturing me and yourself. Say what's in your heart."

"I'm falling for her and uh…" Sky shook her head, shocked with herself. "I don't know how I got here." Her eyes widened, overwhelmed and in need of a drink. "I've been denying any attraction to this woman and okay, the truth is… initially I wasn't attracted to her. She is her and I am me. But the more I see her, the more *I see her.*" Sky's confusion began to turn into a migraine, unable to see the path to how she came to this moment.

She had gone from never considering Eva as an option to longing for their next encounter.

"I see her in the small things she does that makes me smile. I see her in the dreams I thought were too hard to accomplish. Even with her walls up, it's easy to fall in love with her. She's not trying to be perfect or whining if she's uncomfortable. She's just trying to live in a way that leaves her happy."

Sky had been staring down at her hands, consumed with all these feelings spilling out. When she looked up, she found her dad watching her with a grin.

"What?"

"Why are you here?" he asked.

Sky frowned. "Because…" She needed to sort through her feelings and came for her dad's help. But he hadn't said a word as she sorted through them herself. Sky realized that there was more to it than that and sighed. "It can't work."

He nodded. "That's where you're struggling. You see all the ways it could go wrong because you're afraid and you still can't accept your feelings for her." Her dad wanted to support whatever choice she made but he knew she needed tough love. "You've always had this idea of the perfect partner and after your mother passed, it changed but you still hold on to an image. And it's not realistic, honey. Either you want an honest, passionate, long-lasting love or you don't."

Sky sighed.

"The easy part is over. You've acknowledged your feelings. The hard part is owning it. And of course, it would be nice if Eva felt the same way," he said.

Sky groaned exaggeratedly.

"She's barely talking to me again. I don't want to screw things up."

"How about you focus on being her friend first? And when the time is right, you'll know."

That was great advice.

A nurse appeared in the doorway. Sky stood and hugged her dad.

"Thanks. I can sleep now."

He laughed. "Go home. Drink some tea and tomorrow will be a brand-new beginning."

Sky would have to find some faith by the morning if she was going to face Eva again. A lot of faith.

Chapter Twenty

Eva spent the entire weekend at home working on the redesign of one of her client's websites, highly aware that she was avoiding going into town. Now that it was Monday, Eva couldn't pretend she was invisible anymore. Opening up to Sky a few nights back had been hard and intimidating but she'd made Eva feel good about her choice in sharing something hard from her past. But part of Eva was now concerned Sky would act differently toward her and Eva wouldn't be able to handle that.

The students were rehearsing their lines when Eva stepped into the room. Chas and Sky were talking at his desk and seemed to be in deep conversation, not noticing her walk in. She didn't want to intrude, the conversation obviously private, and decided to observe what the students were doing.

She pulled out her sketchbook, finding a spot in a corner and waited until she saw something that inspired her to draw. She sat in peaceful silence until she heard her name called. Chas waved for her to come over and Eva noticed the eager smile on Sky's face and got up.

"I didn't want to disturb you guys." Eva sat in the chair beside Sky, shifting a few times from her jeans brushing up uncomfortable sensations.

Sky's brow arched whimsically.

"You doing okay over there?" she teased.

Eva averted her head shyly.

"Uh, yeah. Just a conflict with these jeans."

"Need help?" Sky offered.

Eva's head shot up, confused by her offer.

Sky stuttered, blushing, "No. I meant that I could oh, loosen them and give you some wiggle room in the crotch region." Sky realized how ridiculous she sounded and wanted to hide behind something bigger than a rock.

Chas studied Sky impassively as Eva stared with her own inquisitions.

"Chas and I were just going over the creations I've done so far for the student's costumes, and we were thinking of a unique way of getting the materials, cost efficient," Sky explained.

"Unfortunately, the school can't afford to give us more than what was placed in our budget." Chas looked exhausted, as if he'd been working on the issue all weekend.

Eva didn't want to be invasive. She'd only come here with the intention of doing the bare minimum, but she'd grown to care for the success of the program and the students.

"If you don't mind me asking, with everything you need for this play to be a big success, how much would you need?"

There was hesitation as Chas furrowed his brows, contemplating how he should answer.

"We can't help you figure this out if we don't have a realistic number to go off," Sky said, encouraging him to open up. "We volunteered to help because we want these students to get exactly what they deserve. And what you've worked so hard for."

Eva sat back and waited for Chas to decide. She could relate to his anxiety over asking for help. It wasn't easy leaning on others, and in the past, there'd been no one.

He frowned but nodded.

"Roughly $3,500 more."

Sky nodded. "Okay!"

"Before you say that we should go around town asking for donations, no!" Chas was adamant. "I love this town, but there are still some out there who are conservative and want to see me fail. I won't beg them."

"But this isn't just about you, and no one said anything about begging," Sky spoke softly, giving Chas a stern look of chastisement. "Let go of that pride. At the end of the day, it will be the play that does the talking."

Chas huffed and rolled his eyes.

While Sky and Chas were having a staring match, Eva had made a decision of her own.

"Does the theatre program have its own funding account or do all things just come through the school itself?"

Chas frowned dubiously. "We have our own funding account that I have access to. The school usually just adds the money into the account every semester."

Eva went back to what she was doing, writing down what was needed.

"Eva…" Sky's voice came out as a whisper.

"Here." Eva held the check out and slid it across Chas's desk. "I made it an even four grand."

Chas eyes widened. "No!"

"I either give it to you, and you put it into the account, or I take it to the principal or whoever's in charge of it and they do it anyway." When Eva was passionate about something, there was no talking her out of it. It was only a matter of Chas accepting the check or the school. "I promised myself that once I was financially successful, I'd make it a priority to give back to my community and I haven't done that yet. You've given me the space to finally do it now. So, let me."

She could see the tears forming in his eyes. Chas averted his head and grabbed a Kleenex to dab the corner of his eye and groaned quietly. He shook his head before looking up with heavy emotion.

"Can I give you a hug? And you have to say yes!"

Eva wasn't accustomed to an open display of affection but if Chas could accept her gift, then she could accept his gratitude and what that came with.

"First time for everything."

He stood and moved around the desk, and she got up just as he reached in for a hug. She didn't know what to do with her hands, so she patted his back and he laughed.

"You better get used to this! We're all about showing love and affection in this group," Chas said, chuckling.

After several heartbeats, they parted ways, some of the students coming over with curious expressions.

Chasity smiled and exchanged looks with all of them.

"What's happening?"

Chas squeezed Eva's shoulder gently and answered.

"Well Eva here, just donated money for our theater production. So that speech I gave you all last week—you can forget that." He looked at Sky and Eva to explain what he'd told his students. "I shared with them on Friday the limitations our budget was under. They deserved to know what was going on."

"Also teaches them the unfortunate necessity of money," Eva added.

Sky crossed her arms and narrowed her eyes.

"You had to add that in there?"

Eva shrugged. "It's the truth."

"Everyone, thank Eva for her generosity," Chas said as he gained his students' full attention.

Many approached, showing their appreciation, Chasity walking up last.

Eva smiled at Chasity.

"Would you like to be the first person I do a portrait of?"

Chasity's eyes widened.

"Really? Yes." They skipped toward where Eva normally sat.

"I should get to it." Eva nodded and walked off before Sky and Chas could say a word.

She'd needed an escape and Chasity was the way out. Eva couldn't handle too much praise, her only goal was to help and get back to why she was here.

Eva took a seat in her usual spot, legs crossed, opening her sketchbook. She didn't know why but she looked up to find Sky watching her and smiled. Sky smiled back and it left a warm feeling in her chest.

Sketching Chasity would be a much-needed distraction. Eva asked Chasity a few questions to get them comfortable with being drawn and studied the outside of their face before she started.

They twisted in their chair, discomfort growing with every second that passed. Sky noticed Chasity's unique differences from the other students and wanted to make sure Chasity knew they were in a safe space. If Eva was going to get Chasity to relax, she had to be vulnerable too.

She placed the pencil on top of her sketchbook, legs crossed as she removed her beanie. Eva had a habit of hiding behind her beanie as if that would prevent her from being seen. Eva ran her fingers through her coiled hair, lips in a straight line as she made brief eye contact.

"I have social anxiety and tend to emotionally tap out and go into hiding when I get overwhelmed." Eva's honesty left a smile on Chasity's face that shined through their eyes.

Chasity's fingers tapped repetitively against their thigh. They stared down at their hands, aware of their movement. When they looked back up, Chasity spoke timidly.

"I have Obsessive Compulsive Disorder. I tap my fingers or foot anytime I am trying to resist the impulse to do something that's more noticeable and potentially disruptive."

"Thank you for sharing," Eva said.

"You shared first." They smiled.

That seemed to be the big icebreaker they needed to relax. Eva picked up the pencil and began sketching. They talked about animation and gaming design for the next thirty minutes until Eva felt a light tap on the shoulder.

Eva stopped drawing and looked up to find Sky standing beside her and noticed the students getting ready to leave.

"It was great bonding with you. I have more than enough to finish."

Chasity tried to sneak a peek, but Eva tilted her sketchbook up, blocking the view.

"Aww. But I really want to see."

"I know. But today, how about practicing patience. I believe in you." Eva smiled and waved at Chasity when they got up to grab their belongings.

"Thanks a million, Ms. Flowers." Chasity looked at their phone and huffed. "My dad's here. I got to go." They stormed out of the room right away.

"You're amazing with them," Sky relished. She looked around nervously before turning back to Eva who was packing her bag. "Umm, would you like to join us for dinner tonight?"

Eva looked past Sky to find Chas sneaking glances their way. There was the temptation to spend more time with Sky but that came with sharing space with others. It was not necessarily being around everyone within Sky's friend group that made it difficult for her. It was her confusion about her connection with Sky and not knowing what she wanted from her.

Eva smiled, keeping her response brief.

"I should get home. I need to finish a few personal projects."

"Okay." Sky tried not to look disappointed. "Well… see you tomorrow."

"Thanks again." One corner of Chas's mouth lifted to a smile as he held his hand out.

Eva shook it, relieved he didn't ask for another hug.

"For the kids."

She left, giving them both a quick wave goodbye without another glance. For only a second, Eva questioned herself, painfully aware she was off to hide again.

Denise warned her that she'd never fulfill her dream of having a family if she stayed hidden. There weren't a lot of things Eva wanted but the few things she'd longed for were dominated by fear on a regular basis. But with every step Eva took away from making a real connection with someone, the safer she felt. It was a twisted existence, she acknowledged, but one she didn't know how to break out of. A problem to solve tomorrow.

Chapter Twenty-One

For the next two weeks, rehearsals were held in the main theater room. Most of the students had their lines memorized, less than a month away from their performance the week of Valentine's Day. Though the play would be mostly dramatic with a twist of mild romance and sneaky humor, it still had a symbolic message that would feel almost like a Hallmark ending. The protagonist would live peacefully, with no need to ever fight away evil again. Only brightness would fill the ambiance and leave the audience feeling hopeful and inspired.

Sky finished all the measurements for the students' costumes, getting the right material needed. She'd be done with their designs in another week, and then it was a matter of making small adjustments.

"Pause!" Chas held his hand up, skipping up the steps to the stage where one of his main cast members stood, pretending to be terrified, leaning against the wall. She portrayed Mina who was psychically connected to Dracula.

Everyone stayed in their positions as Chas explained the emotion she needed to exhibit for her reaction to be felt by the audience. Once he was finished, he announced a break and they dispersed.

Sky shaded blue into a drawing she made of one of the students' costumes. She was consumed with finishing and startled when Chas snuck up from behind. Sky nearly ruined the drawing, glancing sternly at Chas with warning.

He laughed and lifted both hands in surrender.

"My bad. Don't beat me up."

"You are a…" a few of the students were close enough to hear so she edited her words, "butt head."

Chas laughed. "Yep!" He sat beside her and watched her finish. "Any progress with Eva? I know I've been busy. I'm sorry I haven't checked in."

Sky sighed and looked up, aware of where Eva was in the room.

"We've met up several times to go over the art portfolio. Small conversations but she won't drop her walls completely. It's still just surface level."

He nodded and frowned.

"Maybe you should do what your father suggested in the beginning."

"What?" Sky's dad had a lot of suggestions.

"Let her draw a portrait of you," Chas said. "Expose yourself and I guarantee she'll be likely swayed to do the same."

Sky considered, brows knitting together as she wavered if it was worth trying, only to be stuck with Eva in awkward silence the entire time.

"Either try or continue to do what you're doing now. Nothing." Chas pulled out his phone and groaned.

"Everything okay?" Sky asked.

"Yep. Just the usual. A boy who can't be a man." He turned off his phone and slid it back into his pocket. He looked at Sky with a gentle smile. "Ask yourself this at least, why persist if you're only going to leave after the productions are over? Your dad's recovery is going well, and he'll be back home in a week. Why continue if you have no desire to accept how you feel about her?"

Sky stared down at her drawing, confronted with choices she'd forced to the back of her mind. Sky never backed down from a challenge, but it seemed she'd met her match. Eva was all the things Sky never pictured for herself but if she was being honest with herself, Eva was all the things she needed. But her career mattered too, and she couldn't see that growing here.

But Sky wasn't exactly working the gigs she wanted back in the city either. If she was honest with herself, she could admit she'd been doing more here.

"Make up your mind fast." Chas stood, hunching over her. "She's packing to leave," he whispered and kissed her forehead before clapping his hands together to gather the students back.

Sky watched Eva collect her belongings and stand to leave. Sky's hesitation lasted a few seconds, and she rushed across the theater room just as Eva moved to leave.

"You have time to draw me?"

Eva was surprised to find Sky standing beside her with an anxious demeanor.

"Uh… now?"

Sky cleared her throat and tried to sound confident.

"You've sketched every student, including Chas. I thought it was time I got my portrait done."

Eva looked around and then at her backpack on the chair. "I guess I can do it now. If that's what you want."

"I do," Sky nodded. "It is." She sat down and waited for Eva to do the same.

"Okay." Eva pinched the bridge of her nose and settled back into the chair. She pulled out her larger sketchbook and two pencils, sharpening one of them. Her gaze lingered on the blank white paper, unable to draw a line. "Maybe we should—"

"Will you ever let me in?" Sky asked in a desperate tone. If something was on her mind, she needed to understand. "I'm trying to let you in. I'm trying right now."

Eva sighed and finally lifted her head long enough to look into Sky's eyes. She pulled off her beanie and stared pensively at her as if trying to decide what to say.

"Do you want me to draw you with the scarf on?"

Sky looked down, having forgotten she was wearing it and removed it. She straightened the collar on her blouse and looked up, more exposed than she was before. Sky swallowed and nodded to signal she was ready.

For a long time, Eva studied her as if really seeing her for the first time.

Sky froze, heart pounding as Eva reached out to curl one of her dreads behind her ear. She closed her eyes, stifling a deep sigh from Eva's fingertips brushing the side of her neck. When Sky opened them again, she found Eva watching her closely.

Sky cleared her throat.

"Thank you," she said in a raspy voice.

Eva nodded. When their gaze broke, she grabbed her pencil and began sketching her.

It was hard being drawn by Eva, who could acknowledge all Sky's imperfections free of charge. Every time Eva looked up to find some new part of Sky to sketch, it was as if she was looking into her soul. Sky wanted to cover her face and forget the whole thing but that would mean she was running. But Sky still didn't ask herself what she wanted. How could she expect Eva to open up if she didn't give her a reason to?

The minutes drifted by slowly and by the time Eva was finished, all the students had left. Eva was already packing her things to leave, and Sky had been stuck frozen in her head for a while. She couldn't let the day end and not say something that could change the dynamic of their relationship.

"Are you hungry?" Sky asked.

Eva frowned. "I should…" Eva paused, nibbling on her bottom lip in contemplation and looked back up. "I don't know how to do this."

Sky nodded. "That's okay. Can you just trust me long enough to follow my lead?"

Eva's brows knitted together, and she nodded.

"Okay."

"Dinner at the bar. Just me and you." Sky knew Eva wasn't ready for a social gathering, every encounter not being an exciting one so far.

It took less than ten minutes to reach the bar, finding a booth tucked in a corner near the entrance. Sky grabbed the menus from the counter and sat across from Eva who seemed to be rethinking coming here. Sky reached across the table, placing her hand over Eva's to reassure her that she'd made the right decision.

"It would hurt if you left."

Eva glanced down at their hands and then up at Sky as if deliberating their future.

"Why are you working so hard to be my friend? It can't be because of your dad. And you're leaving soon."

It seemed Eva wanted to jump straight into the hard topics, Sky hadn't still answered for herself. How vulnerable did she have to be to get Eva to do the same? Sky hadn't planned on telling her anything but now, she could see that would likely be the only way for Eva to stay and try to work through the awkward tension.

Sky squeezed her eyes shut, the heaviness in her chest increasing. As she exhaled,

Sky spoke, needing to just be honest and stop stalling.

"I kissed you because I like you." Once Sky said the words, she couldn't seem to stop saying it all. "At the time, I didn't think about the why, I just reacted and I'm sorry for not... respecting your boundaries and I swear, I do not drink like that a lot, and it will never happen again."

Sky couldn't stress enough how embarrassed and regretful she was toward Eva that night.

"But please know, I would have kissed you even if you were wearing that Game of Thrones sweater."

She smiled and felt the pressure in her chest ease. She looked down at their fingers still linked, grateful Eva hadn't pulled away.

"Every time I'm with you, I feel like it's never enough. The truth is... I was arrogant in what I considered near perfection from a partner. You're not what I expected. I've been struggling these last few weeks being near you but not able to talk to you the way I would like to. I—"

"Hey, ladies!" Keith had the worse timing ever. He stood beside them with a beer bottle in hand and without permission sat beside Sky, forcing her to shift further into the booth. "I couldn't help but overhear your speech, and I felt let like it was my civil duty to prevent you from making a bigger full out of yourself. I mean, come on!" He flung his hand out toward Eva in a dismissive gesture. "It's her!" he said, dramatically. "You can't be serious. You're one of the most gorgeous women in town. If you're going to be gay, at least find someone who matches your charm and good looks." Keith winked and playfully bumped his shoulder against Sky as if she'd find him funny.

Sky exhaled slowly and shut her eyes before she spoke. If she was like anyone, it was her father when it came to handling assholes.

"If you don't mind, I was just telling Eva that I am falling for her and you're ruining it by being a piece of shit right now."

Sky chanced sneaking a peek at Eva, who looked ready to bolt.

Keith stared dumbfounded with his mouth hung open.

"You're serious?"

"Keith. How about you figure out how much longer you plan to be an asshole before life slips by and you're alone in the end?" Eva spoke calmly but there was no mistaking the sternness in her voice.

It seemed whatever impression Keith wanted to make wouldn't be working out and he stood, embarrassed.

"Uh, I was..." he sighed, looked down at the beer in his hand and frowned. "My drunk ass deserved that. I'm sorry." He nodded and stormed out of the bar, leaving his bottle on the counter.

They were met with silence and a few looks from neighboring tables. Eva looked ready to run.

Sky wouldn't let a second slip away without getting her words out.

"I know we're different. And before a few weeks ago, I thought maybe we were too different. But I know deep down that doesn't have to matter. I've seen successful relationships between two totally different people. I also know there's the question of me heading back to the city and the truth is, I don't know at this point what I'm going to do. All I know is… I would like to go out on a date with you. So, will you?"

Eva studied Sky for the longest time. She'd been asked before but had been too focused on being judged to give her past relationships a real chance. Somehow saying no to Sky would feel like the wrong choice. Maybe it was time to take a risk. She hadn't allowed herself to think of Sky as anything other than Mr. Wyman's daughter. Eva didn't know how she felt about her, but she wanted to find out.

"The suspense is killing me." Sky impatiently narrowed her eyes as if it would help pull an answer out of Eva.

"I must be tripping to think this is even a good idea." Eva frowned and sucked in a considerably long breath, searching for anything that could tell her going out with Sky was a good idea. "Do you really think this is a good idea? I don't want to make any future interactions awkward if it doesn't work out. I care about your dad. And I care about being your friend. I know I haven't done a good job of showing it, but I do."

Sky could dwell on the what ifs and fear the possible negative outcomes or trust that the connection they had might work out. She was tired of lying to herself and wanted to find out how far she could fall for Eva. Sky reached across the table again, lacing their fingers together with more confidence than before.

"I want to try but only if you want to."

Eva studied Sky for the longest time before a smile crept into the corner of her lips.

"Then let's try."

Giddiness swept over Sky's entire body, about ready to leap out of the booth, a huge smile spreading across her face.

"And to be clear... I don't want to hide it from anyone. Are you okay with that?"

Eva nodded. "I expected as much. No more hiding."

"Good."

Chapter Twenty-Two

"Are you really ready for this?" Sabrina sat on the couch watching Eva decide between which shoes to wear.

Denise sat quietly beside her, sipping her glass of wine, unable to say anything. Friday had come full circle; the last couple days working beside Sky during rehearsal felt easy and fun. Eva had been more relaxed in the open than ever.

She was already nervous about tonight and her friends weren't helping. She held both shoes, standing in front of them impatiently.

"You both told me to stop hiding. I listened. You should be proud of me."

Sabrina got to her feet and reached out to squeeze Eva's arm in a show of support.

"Hey! We are happy for you. This is a big step." She smiled and looked at both shoes, picking the black boots with teddy bears stitched in tan and white along the sides.

"Thanks." Eva sat on the ottoman to put on the boots, with black skinny jeans and a tan button-up shirt, and her light blue sweatshirt that had a computer circuit printed in tan on the front.

"You trying to scream nerd?" Denise asked, scrutinizing her outfit.

Eva squinted her eyes, trying to get a read on Denise's emotions. Though there had been a clear acceptance in moving forward as friends, Eva didn't think this was easy for Denise and wanted to be mindful of her feelings.

"I'm trying to be me."

"Sky knows who she's going out with. You look amazing," Sabrina complimented, while failing to sneak a chastising look at Denise who seemed unaware.

"I know this is unexpected." Eva reached for her beanie and put it on. "But... I do want to try. I've enjoyed getting to know Sky. I want to see if this is real or if I just like how she makes me feel in the moment."

"That's real," Sabrina agreed. "I love this for you."

"Thanks," Eva said. She looked at Denise, trying to read her thoughts.

Denise sighed. "We... I don't want you to jump in too deep, too fast. I'm afraid if things don't go the way you hope, they might do more than put you back in hiding. It might isolate you completely from us."

Eva could see where Denise's fear came from and wanted to reassure them both. But, as she opened her mouth to promise them nothing would make her lose all the progress she was making, she knew how unrealistic of a promise that was.

She thought of something honest and promising to say.

"I will never walk away from you two. I know I don't say this enough, but I need you in my life. I would not be as open as I am trying to be now, if not for your love and encouragement." Eva held both her hands out, and each of them took one. "I want to give you both more. I have been very selfish and one-sided in our friendship and that's going to change. I promise."

Denise and Sabrina found themselves smiling as they stood to have a group hug.

Playfully, Denise tugged at the beanie Eva was wearing.

"Make sure when you get to wherever y'all are going, to take that off," she said adamantly.

"What? Why?" Eva loved wearing her beanies.

Sabrina laughed and nodded in agreement.

"No amount of acceptance will ever make Sky want to see that beanie on your head. Not even us, and we know we love you."

They all laughed.

"Besides," Denise said, finally sounding like her cheerful self. "I've seen the way she looks at you. Let her see all of you."

"Well, not all of you," Sabrina corrected. "At least not tonight. Take your time."

"Okay, mom," Eva joked.

It felt good, sharing this moment with them. Eva had told herself for too long to never expect family to come into her life, and not until now did she realize she'd had it all along in them.

"I love you both!" she said, grateful to have them.

"I love you too," Sabrina said, kissing Eva on the cheek as Denise kissed her on the opposite side.

Denise gave her a warm smile.

"I love you too."

*

There were only two museums in town, one of them also an art gallery. Eva frequented the museums bi-monthly and knew the art gallery was hosting a private showing of a photographer who specialized in unique human art, through makeup, styles, cultural differences, and body poses.

It made her think of Sky and the way she was fascinated with taking mundane looks and creating uniqueness and Eva knew tonight would help feed her passion as a cosmetic artist. It amazed Eva how much effort she put into planning the first half of their date. Eva didn't think she had it in her to be so creative in planning a date.

They'd both agreed to split the responsibility of their date tonight, Sky responsible for planning the second half. They were total opposites, and it gave them the space to share a piece of themselves.

Eva knocked on the door, expecting to find Sky on the other end. When it opened, Frank was standing there, hunched over on a walker.

"What the heck are you doing answering the door?" Eva immediately reached for the door to prop it open so that she could step through and pointed him toward the living room.

He frowned. "You sound like a child of mine," he joked.

That made Eva smile. She guided him to the couch, his pace slow and careful. She grabbed one of his arms, helping him sit. He groaned, relieved to be off his feet.

"I was practicing moving around on my own. Sky won't be here forever, or my health aide," he grumbled.

Eva's smile decreased and he noticed.

"I'm sorry." He smiled and reached out to squeeze her hand. "I wouldn't have encouraged you two so much if I didn't think you two could work."

Eva had no reason to act surprised. She'd decided to go on a date, knowing Sky couldn't guarantee she'd be here next week. And as Eva stood in her feelings, reminded of her circumstances and the chances of getting hurt at the end, she was content with following through.

She let go of her doubts and smiled. "I want to understand where my feelings for your daughter are coming from. I've never fought for my own happiness before."

He shook his head, opposed to her words.

"You fought for your success and the life you have now. How many people do you know can share your story?"

Eva never considered it that way. She had dreams of not relying on others to create her happiness and to put a roof over her head and yet she knew it would be facing people that would be her real challenge. Facing others' acceptance and love for her, without hesitation or selfishness.

She heard Sky coming down the stairs and turned to face that direction, giving Frank a considerate look. When Sky came into view, Eva stared breathlessly, unprepared for how felt. She was struck by a need that hadn't been awakened in years. The desire to touch, feel, experience life with someone else. The need to be loved and wanted and seen. She suddenly pictured it all with Sky and that scared her.

Eva took a step forward, the palms of her hands sweaty and offered Sky the container of cookies she had baked earlier in the day.

"Uh… I know you don't like flowers, so I figured you might like this instead."

"How unoriginal but very old school?" Frank chuckled.

"Dad. Hush and act like you aren't here please." Sky was blushing and he wasn't helping. Sky stood, nervous despite her initial confidence coming down the stairs. She'd used three strands of her dreads and twisted them to make a bun. Dark eyeliner and lipstick highlighted her features. Sky wore black leather fitted pants with a dark red blouse that cut down between her breasts.

Eva didn't know where to look, afraid she'd offend Sky if she stared too long.

"I know you love my cookies." She didn't know what else to say, smiling awkwardly.

"I do!" Sky whispered. She was aware of her dad watching with a grin. He could at least pretend not to pay attention.

It took Sky a second to blur her dad from her peripheral vision and take in every inch of Eva.

"You look really nice."

Eva looked down at herself, self-consciously.

"Too nerdy, huh?"

Sky's lips curved upward as she took a step forward and kissed Eva on the cheek. She lingered for a second, smelling Eva's body spray.

"You look like you and that's who I asked for. You." She stepped away, her own perfume clinging close to Eva, and took the cookies. "Let me hide these from my dad. I'll be right back."

Eva nearly lost her durability to stand. She watched Sky walk away and closed her eyes, feeling the lingering effects of Sky's kiss.

"Take off that silly beanie," Frank muttered. "And cool yourself off. You're melting."

Eva turned to him and narrowed her eyes. She would not feed into the latter of his comment.

"What's wrong with my beanie?"

"It doesn't fit the theme of tonight... being a date," he said, sarcastically. "Surprise her a little. You know that matters to her," Frank said insistently.

Sky lived a very glamorous lifestyle back in the city and her image was a part of her living as a makeup artist for models. Sky loved dressing up, luxury living and high-quality was something she took pleasure in. Eva didn't care for those kinds of things, but they didn't go against any of her core values. As long as Sky didn't expect her to dress up all the time, it was something she could do for her.

So, Eva reached for the beanie and tossed it at Frank playfully.

"When you're right, you're right."

Sky walked back into the living room.

"You ready?" Her eyes widened at the sight of Eva's curly hair wildly free. She had a fresh undercut and trim that left her with only a few inches of hair. "I love seeing your hair like that."

"Stay a while longer?" Frank asked. "I haven't seen you in almost a week."

Sky opened her mouth to argue but noticed his smirk and groaned.

"You are not funny." She offered her hand out for Eva to take. "Ready, or do you want some more alone time with Dad?"

Eva smiled. "Sorry, Frank. I promise to come by Sunday."

He whined impishly.

"Fine. Just make sure she's home by curfew."

"Har, har!" Sky laughed as Eva took her hand and guided her out of the house. "See you later, Dad. Your health aide will be here in twenty minutes."

They left the house, nervous and excited to go on their date.

Chapter Twenty-Three

"When did they upgrade this museum? I don't remember there being an art gallery here before." Sky walked closely next to Eva, instantly captivated by the photography propped on an easel at the front entrance. She looked ahead to see there was a decent crowd inside, some of the people she recognized in town.

Eva loved seeing Sky smile with so much eagerness to see everything inside.

"They added this part a year ago. It's been a popular place to come ever since."

The gallery was a decent size, allowing enough art and imagination to fill up the place and bring in a crowd. The walls were painted off-white which helped make the art in the room stand out and be seen. Instead of the big bright overhead lights being on, the gallery had electric candle lights lit throughout, making it a dim and intimate space. They were showcasing one artist tonight, their art hung on walls and easels.

"Well damn. I'm glad they thought of this. We have more culture here than the big city I live in," Sky said.

Eva wanted to dig into Sky's reasons to stay in the city, if only to understand rather than pretend there wasn't a place she would go back to.

"Other than going back for your career, what else do you love about the city?"

They walked along the gallery wall, Sky stopping short of a photo that kept her staring, mesmerized. The black woman in the photo sat naked on the floor, slumped and exhausted, as if life had won too many rounds against her. Instead of actual tears, they were painted on her face in gold. Her skin was covered with words painted over her to represent all her hardships.

Sky looked over to see the same woman in a different position, with anger in her eyes and tears smeared over her face.

"He's telling a story. See?"

Eva's eyes followed the large, bold images, seeing the representation of every black woman's struggle to be weighed down and then using pure will and determination to overcome and stand tall and independent from any man. She smiled, impressed by the artist's work.

"They have one art gallery in the city. Can you believe that? Only one, with maybe two museums, and small libraries with not enough books. The city does not value art and knowledge the way I thought any big city would." Sky made it to the end of the series and sighed. "That was a beautiful collection. If this series was amazing, I can imagine the rest."

Eva grinned. "I'm glad you're enjoying yourself."

Sky moved to walk but stopped and looked at Eva with so much affection.

"I mostly stay in the city for work. I have a few friends out there and I love the food, though it's expensive as hell. But that's it." Sky closed the distance between them. "Thank you for bringing me here. I can see the core things we love; we have in common. Art."

"Mhm." Eva wasn't used to showing a display of affection in public but if Sky wanted to kiss her right now, she would not say no.

Sky smiled flirtatiously. The way Eva looked at her, it was the first time she felt confident that Eva was feeling the same thing. Finally, she could see it and that made her happy. Sky had the urge to lick her lips; instead, she nibbled lightly on the inner skin.

"Come on. We have much more to see."

She slid her hand into Eva's and guided them into the next series of photography.

Eva's cheeks flushed; Sky's hand was soft around hers in a gentle grip. There was pride and happiness, standing beside Sky. After all the years Eva had stayed hidden away, she now understood how it felt to want to be seen with someone she cared about. Her perspective was changing as she experienced it.

"What are you thinking about?" Sky pivoted back to stand closer and tilted her head at Eva with curiosity.

"I uh…" Eva ran her fingers through her hair nervously and looked around.

Sky whispered. "Is this too much?" She looked down at their fingers, still linked.

"Oh, no!" Eva leaned forward, instinctively wanting to reassure Sky that there was nothing wrong. "I was thinking about how much my life has changed in such a short time."

Sky nodded, cognizant of Eva's life before meeting her.

"Do you feel like it's still your life or someone else you're pretending to be?"

The question was sincere and realistic to Eva's circumstances.

"I feel like it's still me, just two-point-oh, I guess." Eva pondered internally, wanting a better answer, at least for herself. Her reasons for staying private and secluded were still there but Sky had given her newfound curiosity to step out of her comfort zone. And it felt nice being able to walk amongst her neighbor's and not feel invisible. "I told myself, if I did things on my own, no one would be able to hurt or judge me. Or at least I won't be around to hear or feel it." Eva shrugged.

"But deep down… I've always longed to be a part of something greater than myself. Working with those kids has given me more in life than I'd been giving myself in the last decade." Eva looked into Sky's eyes, confident and relaxed. "I'm happy."

They gazed into each other's eyes, swept away by emotion that was sweet and comfortable. There were no words that needed to be said, both their expressions conveying a yearning to grow closer.

"Ladies."

Their private moment was cut short by an older woman standing beside them.

Eva smiled at Sky before turning to observe the woman standing poised, in a long stylish coat and fur hat. Mrs. Grayson was in her late fifties, brown-toned, with a pensive look in her eyes.

"I thought that was the two of you." Mrs. Grayson tilted her head back, openly acknowledging their fingers laced together. "On a date, I presume?"

There wasn't a look of judgement or surprise in seeing Sky holding hands with Eva, the tech nerd loner. It felt good, being seen without amusement in her presence.

"Yes ma'am." Sky responded gleefully, leaning casually into Eva as if she'd done so hundreds of times. "Eva had the brilliant idea to bring me here, and I love it."

Mrs. Grayson bowed her head, gesturing to Eva in admiration of her choice of location for a date.

"I actually met the artist at a convention in the city and suggested to the gallery to host her work."

"Really?" Sky asked, intrigued. "Perhaps we can get a V.I.P introduction at the end of the show."

"Of course! Perhaps, if you moved back, you might be able to get exclusive access to any artist who passes through. And who knows, your career might be better suited here in town," Mrs. Grayson said casually.

Sky laughed. "You've been conversing with my dad, I see!" she joked.

Mrs. Greyson shrugged.

"Slightly." She squinted her eyes at Eva and smiled. "I hear you are quite the artist. I look forward to seeing the portfolio you two create for the school play."

"I'm all right," Eva said awkwardly.

Sky shook her head and gave Eva a silly look.

"All right. No! She's—her art needs to be seen." There weren't enough words to convey how amazing Eva was as an artist.

Mrs. Grayson studied Eva and nodded.

"I will see soon enough but I have no doubt your art is of high quality. Remember," Mrs. Grayson tapped her temple. "You were in my art classes too."

Eva smiled. "I remember."

"Have you ever considered getting your teaching license or something equivalent to that? I retire at the end of school year," Mrs. Grayson asked.

Eva didn't expect Mrs. Grayson to potentially offer her job. She stared, surprised by her question.

"Uh…"

"She's been stubborn about it but I'm sure with your recommendation, she'd consider," Sky spoke up in her place.

"Well, after working at that high school for almost thirty years, they'd let me pick whoever I wanted even if they only knew how to paint stick figures," Mrs. Grayson joked. She looked up and pouted. "My husband is getting restless without me." She reached out to squeeze both their arms. "You two are on a date. But how about we talk after the play. I think you'd benefit the school more than you know."

"Thank you, Mrs. Grayson," Sky said.

"Have a great night." Eva smiled and watched her walk away. When she turned to face Sky, there was a cheesy grin on her face. "I never said I'd take the job. I have a lot on my plate."

Sky moved in front of Eva and shook her playfully. "I know if you really took a moment and considered, you'd make room for it if you wanted to." Sky smiled and looked towards the wall where more art was displayed. "Come on! We still have lots to see."

It would be a huge change if Eva took a job at the high school. There would be no more hiding. She'd have to deal with teens and their parents on a regular basis. She'd have to interact and make conversation with staff, some of whom were teachers when she was in high school and had treated her poorly. There was a lot to think about but for now, Eva would put it in the back of her mind.

Eva was on a date, and she wanted to experience every moment of it.

*

After the art gallery, Sky wanted to take Eva to her favorite spot. It was a small café that had been around since she was a kid. It sat at the top of a small mountain, next to a creek that overlooked the town.

They sat next to a wall-sized window with a scenic view. For the past hour, they had eaten and talked about everything, neither one tired nor ready to go.

Eva sat across from Sky, who was twirling her wine glass and staring peacefully out the window. Sky looked serene, entranced by the view.

Several heartbeats later, Sky shifted a glance to Eva and smiled.

"Mm." Sky had been thinking about the past. "My parents would bring us here on special occasions. Which was often." Sky laughed, reliving those moments.

She sighed. "My mom—she always found a reason for us to come here. If one of us got good grades, it was a special occasion. If we none of us went a week without fighting. Special occasion." Sky smiled, finding Eva watching her closely.

Sky could really see how attentive Eva was, feeling safe to share. The world could come crashing down and Eva would still have her full attention and that felt good.

"When we lost her…"

Sky could feel tears sliding down her face before she could wipe them away, and Eva leaned across the table, catching another tear with her thumb, her touch gentle and kind.

After a moment, Eva moved to drop her hand, but Sky pressed hers over Eva's, wanting to feel her touch a while longer. Sky took in a long breath and relaxed.

"My mom would have loved you. You both... have this ability to make someone feel seen and heard. You're thoughtful and love the outdoors. She was social but she also loved her alone time and would go off hiking or on trips alone. That's something I always admired about her. Fearless when it came to self-care and teaching us it was okay to ask for things you need. I never thought about what that looked like for me and whoever I settled down with. Not until you."

"And she could cook?" Eva grinned.

Sky laughed. "Yes, but she couldn't bake like you."

Sky continued to hold Eva's hand, bringing it down to the table. Her heart swelled at the thought of losing Eva before she could really experience the love shared between the two of them.

"I've always wanted the kind of love I witnessed my parents have. I hope you know, there's nothing I'd ever want to change about you. Even if... you didn't take the teaching job or start going on out to bars on the regular."

"You like a lot of things I've never even bothered to experience or have," Eva pointed out. "And you thrive off the social scene. I want to respect your desires and dreams, and my own." Eva wouldn't pretend she could suddenly enjoy doing all the things Sky liked to do, but she could offer something honest. "I know a great deal of my reasons for not going out have more to do with my fear of being overlooked or judged rather than social anxiety. It's going to take time for me to adjust, but I want to try. I deserve to do better for myself, and the people close to me."

"I love that for you!" Sky agreed. "I promise, I don't want you to ever feel like you're forced to do something. I want you to want to do it."

Eva nodded. "Thank you. I know that growth comes from being uncomfortable sometimes. Doing things you don't want to do. I am willing to experience that because I don't want to give up on what we could have."

"Is the lifestyle here the only reason why you stay? For peace and quiet. Nature. Less people," Sky asked. She wanted to be sure that her instincts were right, that Eva would never leave.

"All that." Eva had never dug in as to why she came back after partially finishing college. She blamed her reasons on the loudness that came with big city life and her insecurities not changing based on location. She smiled timidly, self-conscious of what she'd known to be the truth.

Sky squeezed her hand, sensing Eva's hesitation.

"You don't have to share if you aren't ready to."

"I appreciate that." Eva smiled. "In the beginning, I told myself I'd come back and be a totally different person. I'd shock this town and they'd finally see me for who I am. And then… week one back, I run into old classmates who literally began talking about me in front of my face, shocked that I even came back."

Eva looked down at their fingers intertwined.

"I had an affair with an old classmate… I shouldn't have even entertained. I redesigned her website and one thing led to another, and a week later she told me it was a mistake. After a while, I told myself, what was the point of trying and decided to just stay hidden."

Eva had not thought about her first few years back in so long. It had been a hard time for her.

"The thing is… I always dipped my toe back into the town's water because more than anything I wanted to connect with them. They were all the people I knew. It was like craving the love of a parent who would never give you love in return." Eva shrugged. "I stayed for that alone. Hoping to be loved by them one day." Eva knew how foolish she sounded.

"Maybe a lot of people have always loved and wanted to know you but didn't know how to show that." Sky saw the doubt on Eva's face and frowned. "My dad, for starters. Sabrina, Denise. Chas did try to talk to you once, so he counts." Eva smiled as Sky continued. "Maxine. Mrs. Grayson clearly adores and respects you." Sky lowered her eyes before saying more. "Me!" She swallowed her fear.

"You!" Eva repeated.

Sky looked up and nodded. "You think someone can't fall in love without sex being involved?"

"Uh…" Eva took a long breath and repositioned in her seat. "I'm not saying that."

"Or do you think no one can fall in love with you?"

Eva didn't say anything right away. She had been in love once without the person returning it and she knew Denise had been in love with her. But mutual reciprocated love, she had yet to feel that.

"I don't doubt that."

"Don't ever doubt that from me!"

"Is this a statement?" Eva asked, though she was scared to hear the truth.

"Like I said the other day, I've been falling for you long before I knew it. The only thing I'm praying is that… it's enough." Sky did not hesitate to answer.

"You've never been afraid to tell anyone how you felt." Eva smiled.

Sky laughed. "If you are referring to the many times I stated my opinion during class, then, whatever."

Eva laughed too. "Stated your opinion is an understatement. You made sure there was no confusion about what your opinion was. Especially, if you got a grade you disapproved of."

"Well… I fight for what I need!" Sky looked into Eva's eyes and hoped her expression conveyed exactly what she needed from Eva. "I need you to want this too! More than I've ever needed anything, because yes, I am in love with you."

The tension oozing out of Sky could be felt a mile away and it left Eva breathless.

"I'm not a begging woman and I don't think I've ever fought for a relationship in my life." Sky couldn't contain what she felt as she voiced her thoughts fervently. "I denied what I felt for weeks and then tore at my own flaws to see that love doesn't have to make sense right away. And that it takes discomfort to make something grow, as you've stated. All I ask is that you try… and meet me halfway here."

Eva looked into the brown of Sky's eyes and did not doubt the truth. For years, she'd wanted something that would leave her body burning from the inside and heart swelling so big inside her chest that it might suffocate with yearning, unable to diminish. She never knew who that person would be, or who would give her the thing she longed for the most. A family.

She'd become friends with Frank without knowing it would be his daughter she would fall in love with. Eva couldn't say those words yet, something she needed to be sure of. "I never gave myself permission to fall in love with someone I knew could love me back. And I never thought it would be possible to love someone who seemed too good to be true. You are more than I pictured for myself and to feel your love for me… I don't have the words." Eva didn't want to dismiss what Sky had so bravely expressed.

"In English?" Sky smiled, needing clarification.

Eva made a decision and stood, offering her hand out. Sky stared at it, a confused smile on her face.

"Come home with me and let me show you!" Eva's voice was confident, offering so much promise.

Sky shuddered out a breath and took Eva's hand without hesitation.

Eva dropped some cash on the table and escorted Sky out of the restaurant without saying another word, both women aware of what was about to happen. And that was enough to leave their bodies yearning during the entire drive to Eva's home.

Chapter Twenty-Four

"Would you like something to drink? I have wine or water." Eva looked up from the fridge, her body jittery as she looked toward Sky who was standing in the living room.

"Uh…" Sky seemed to be nervous too, struggling to come up with an answer. "Water will be fine."

Eva poured water from the pitcher into two glasses and closed the fridge. She squeezed her eyes shut and let out a long anxious breath, begging some of her confidence to come back.

She walked into the living room, Sky standing in the same spot she was left in. Sky smiled nervously and it sort of helped Eva feel safer, knowing she wasn't the only one scared to make the first move.

"Here you go." Eva handed her the glass and they both drank, their eyes dancing around the living room. Eva moved to the couch, placed the glass on the table, and turned to find Sky checking her out.

Sky laughed. "Sorry," she shook her head, blushing.

"Why?" Eva asked, walking back to her.

"Uh…" Sky tilted the glass to her mouth as if she was going to drink more water and then mumbled, "I was just… examining your… body."

Eva arched a brow.

"Examining. Like… medically examining me with your eyes," she joked.

Sky shook her head and turned away, finding herself blushing.

"Okay. I was checking out your ass. It's… nice."

"Squats," Eva said playfully.

"Huh?"

Eva laughed. "I love doing squats and lunges. I use the stair climber a lot. It helps me for big hikes."

"Makes sense." Sky cleared her throat and nipped on her inner lip. "Anything else you do to prepare for big hikes?" She asked in a playful tone. Eva always wore loose-fitting clothes with not much access to checking her out.

Eva grinned, offering to take Sky's glass. She handed it to Eva, and it was placed on the table. Eva closed the distance between them.

"Before you go asking what other places on my body are hard and smooth, shouldn't you at least confirm if my ass meets your expectations?" Eva offered.

Sky's brows raised at the open invitation to touch her, highly turned on by Eva's flirtatious soft voice. Sky swallowed and looked down, her mouth watering. But Eva went one step further in driving Sky's libido crazy and singularly accomplishing making her wet.

Never taking her eyes off Sky, Eva blindly reached down to unzip her pants and slid them halfway down. She turned, wearing blue briefs and twisted her head, waiting for Sky to touch her.

Eva felt bold and confident, being this way with Sky, knowing she could trust her with her body and heart.

It took Sky only a second to lean in and brush her fingers over Eva's firm tight ass and she exhaled. Eva leaned into her touch and Sky squeezed, causing Eva to moan.

"Is it how you pictured it to be?" Eva asked.

Sky continued to run her hand along Eva's ass and nodded. She had to remember Eva's back was turned and spoke in a rasp.

"Yes."

Eva turned back and was about to pull her pants back up, but Sky grazed her fingernails up Eva's arm. She couldn't stifle her moan and shuddered from Sky's touch.

"Do you have to?" Sky asked breathlessly. Her mouth was inches from Eva's, seconds from giving into desire. She could feel Eva breathing just as heavily, as they both nearly leaned in and closed the distance.

Instead of pulling her pants back up, Eva let them drop to the floor. Eva's clit throbbed and she pressed her legs close together trying to get off on the sensation.

"Can I... continue to explore what else is hard underneath these clothes?" Sky felt like she was begging. Inside, she was.

Eva could only nod.

When Sky's fingers brushed her skin just below her pelvis, Eva jolted and leaned in, kissing Sky passionately, their tongues brushing one another, teeth tugging each other's lips. They moaned in each other's mouths and Eva had to curl one of her arms around Sky's back just to steady herself.

Sky fingers raked across Eva's ass, causing her to moan again. Sky couldn't help herself; the way Eva felt and the sounds she made.

"I've been wanting to touch you like this since we went hiking," she admitted, their mouths parted for only a few seconds.

"Don't stop," Eva panted, bringing one of her hands to cup Sky's cheek. She took a few steps back, pinning Sky against the back end of the couch. Blindly, she reached for Sky's red blouse, pulling it off and being met with a red silk-laced bra.

Eva soaked in every curve and smooth surface of Sky's skin. Sky arched her neck and Eva brushed her lips right above her breast. Eva's hands brushed down Sky's curvy wide hips, squeezing lightly around her thigh, all while grazing her lips around the soft skin of Sky's chest.

Sky's arms closed around Eva's neck, fingers digging into her hair.

"Oh…" she moaned when Eva's teeth tugged at her ear. "Please. I can't…"

It was hard to say what was on her mind, but it didn't matter. Eva knew what she was asking for.

Eva pulled away, removing her sweater and shirt, exposing toned shoulders with long arms that could wrap around Sky any day of the week. Her stomach was smooth, tattoos of symbols going down the left side of her stomach.

It caught Sky by surprise as she stared, confused.

"Tech symbols?" she asked playfully.

Eva snorted. "Even better. *Star Wars* symbols." She shook her head, laughing. "Do you want a *Star Wars* lesson or me?"

Sky leaned in and kissed Eva softly and gently, playing with the earring in her ear. She pulled back far enough for Eva to look into her eyes.

"I want you now and we can watch an episode or whatever of *Star Wars* after."

Eva blushed at her sincerity and kissed her back with equally sensual passion.

"Deal."

They ended up in Eva's bedroom, removing their clothes, Sky on top.

Their kiss was long and passionate, both finding it hard to stop. Eva's fingers grazed up Sky's inner thigh and then up the outer corner of her ass.

"Sky?" Eva whispered, unable to hide her aroused state of mind, voice cracking. Sky lifted her head. "I need to have you." Eva spoke so softly, the shy part of her staring up awkwardly. It was all she could think about, though. Having her come in her mouth.

Sky could see it. The need. Before Sky could move, Eva took Sky by surprise, flipping her onto her back and grinning.

"Two years now of jujitsu!"

"Oh, fuck me... you are full of surprises."

Eva arched her brow.

"Yeah?" She said toothily, shyness gone.

"Yeah." Sky nodded, breathless.

Eva leaned down, giving Sky a rough kiss, and then snatching air from her lungs before sucking Sky's nipple lightly into her mouth.

Eva's fingers slid up her waist, gripping Sky at the curve of her hips. Eva rolled Sky's nipple around in her mouth, flicking ever so lightly at the tip before sucking it back into her mouth. Sky squirmed and moaned, and Eva took that as a sign that she was more than ready.

Sky's fingers raked down Eva's back, begging for her mouth to go down between her legs.

Pleased she was giving her what she wanted, Eva was ready to give Sky what she needed. Her mouth closed over Sky's clit, sucking lightly with her mouth and Sky's hips buckled.

Eva curled an arm around Sky's hips, twirling her tongue around her clit and then down into her pink wet flesh.

"Oh… oh," Sky was already losing it, ass pressing down into the bed and then lifting up.

Eva didn't stop the exploration of finding Sky's most sensitive and earnest spots, tongue diving in and out of her and then over her clit, sucking and twirling until Sky's fingernails were digging into her scalp.

"Fuck… oh," Sky cried out, so incredibly wet, her orgasm building so deep inside she knew if Eva did anything more, she would lose all sense of reality.

And just in time, Eva slid her middle finger inside of Sky while still having her way with her clit, only using the tip of her tongue. Eva didn't mind the squeezing of Sky's legs against her head or the way she twisted around the bed, making Eva chase her movements. Or the way Sky tugged at her hair, moaning for her not to stop.

And Eva didn't. Eva was amorous at the sounds Sky made and the way she said her name. There was no doubting the love in Sky's heart for her and if Eva could do anything, it was to start loving her back.

Sky cried out as her orgasm hit her wave after wave, like an ocean crashing into the surface of land, over and over again. Sky trembled uncontrollably, reaching blinding for Eva to move up.

Their lips met as Sky tasted herself, sighing deeply into Eva's mouth. Eva loved the smell of Sky, as it fueled her own aroused state of mind, needing to be touched and tasted too.

Eva kissed her as Sky's hand cupped her breast.

"I have a feeling we are going to be at this all night. Water, after I make love to you."

Eva lifted up, twisted, and dropped backwards into the bed, wanting Sky's mouth over her.

"Yes ma'am," she said, watching as Sky climbed on top and kissed her with all the love she possessed. And damn, it was a memorable kiss.

Chapter Twenty-Five

Everyone stood on their feet applauding as the students lined up across the stage and bowed their heads. Not one seat in the auditorium was empty as Chas walked up on the stage beside his students. All the hard work invested into the play had paid off. Sky stood beside Eva at the back of the stage.

The last couple of weeks, they'd helped the students with everything they needed, leaving nothing unfinished.

People continued to whistle and clap, until Sky watched Chas lift his hands and reach for the mic resting on the stand.

Some of the students were tearing up and it brought tears to Sky's own eyes seeing how happy and confident they were. These kids received the best and got the praise they deserved.

Sky wiped her tears and Eva reached in, squeezing her hand supportively and not without her own watery eyes.

"This has been…" Chas shook his head, tilting it up to prevent himself from falling apart in front of the crowd. He sighed and looked at each of his students. "You all… shined tonight."

The audience shouted their agreement, and the students leaned into each other, still in their costumes and makeup, now running down some of their faces.

"Many of you have big dreams of being a part of the theater industry and I am so happy, and I know… you guys will be successful!" Chas straightened and laughed. "Okay. Let me take a moment to thank you all for coming and supporting these amazing, talented students. We worked hard and it took more than learning lines and my directive approach. I mean… look at these amazing costumes. Their makeup. It's almost like we had an actual artist design their entire look!"

Sky chuckled, shaking her head.

"He's going to call us out there," she whispered.

"What?" Eva's eyes bulged from their sockets. "No!"

"For the kids. And for yourself." Sky swayed, hoping Eva could see how special a moment this was to celebrate, even for herself.

"And those portfolios with every moment captured. The fun, silly, emotional moments, drawn for all of you to purchase, by the way," Chas snuck in.

Many laughed.

"I swear… I'm no artist, but… it's almost like we do have one who should be in art galleries by now!" Chas was overselling them, and it made Sky want to laugh.

"I want to make sure they get the love and praise they deserve, so can we welcome Sky Wyman and Eva Flowers to the stage?" He looked their way and began waving.

Sky arched a brow, turning to walk backwards as she checked to see if Eva would follow.

"Get your butt out here, Eva," Chas said, outing her.

Eva groaned dramatically and followed Sky across the stage.

Sky could see her nervously looking around as if ready to faint from stage fright and grabbed Eva's hand, guiding her along. The audience began to cheer, standing again as they made it to the center stage, moving beside Chas who reached in for a hug.

"Thank you all again for coming to support this semester's play and we hope to see you at the next one!" Chas moved beside the student nearest him as Sky and Eva did the same.

Each student reached in to hold hands and took one final bow as the audience applauded and the curtains closed.

The moment they were hidden, the students began leaping in the air with wild excitement and hugging each other.

It was overwhelming seeing such joy and Sky stood there watching, knowing she had gotten more out of this than the last three years working in the city.

Eva stood beside her; arms crossed as she spoke softly.

"I remember saying I wanted minimum exposure when I agreed to help out."

Sky turned, brow raised, with an amused smirk on her face.

"You are right. Could you imagine what it would have been like if you had not done more than you intended?"

With a soft laugh, Eva nodded.

"I would have missed out on time spent with you. Or I wouldn't have discovered how much I loved working with kids."

Sky turned and stepped closer.

"Go on?"

Eva rolled her eyes playfully.

"Or experienced the uncomfortable phase that led me to falling in love with you."

"I could kiss you right now," Sky whispered. Eva had finally said the words and it was enough to breathe new life, new possibilities, new dreams, and make them real. "I love you."

Chas stood beside them, clearing his throat.

"The kids are watching."

Sky looked Eva over and let out a deep yearning groan and turned to the students, ready to help them with whatever they needed.

She snuck a peek, noticing Eva watching her and grinned. She'd have her moment later with Eva. For now, she would focus on the students.

*

"Let's hold our shots up to Chas, Sky, and Eva, who did an amazing job for our high school!" Maxine lifted her shot glass as everyone in the bar did the same.

"Cheers!" Someone shouted.

They all drank their shots, while Sky watched Eva pretend to drink hers. She laughed, and took Eva's shot, downing it for her.

They were celebrating, all their friends were here with them tonight.

"You guys really did an amazing job!" Sky's dad stretched his arm out and Sky went in for a hug.

"Thanks, Dad!"

Chas hugged her dad and then Eva reached in for one too.

Sky smiled when she saw her dad kiss Eva on the forehead.

"My girls!" He smiled, pleased with the both of them. Her dad was still recovering but he was now able to walk with a cane. He sat in one of the lower cushion chairs they requested from the bartender, as they all stood between two high tables toward the back of the bar.

"How does it feel to be done?" Sky asked Chas, who was busy eyeing someone across the table.

He grinned. "Girl, please. I still have to teach my regular speech class. But… I am due for a break and glad to be done with the play for this semester."

"I didn't realize all the hard work that went into it. I'm really glad I got to be a part of this with you." Sky reached across the table and squeezed his hand.

"I already bought the portfolio." Denise smiled, looking up at Sky and Eva.

"Me too! It looks amazing," Maxine agreed. "And to think of how y'all started off."

Sky rolled her eyes, sneaking a peak at Eva who was looking down at their hands linked. Sky hadn't realized she had grabbed it.

Sky shifted her glance from Eva, her dad giving his famous *I see everything* look. She could tell he was happy, as if he had been the ringleader to getting her and Eva together. In a way, he deserved the credit. She leaned in and gave her dad a kiss on the cheek. She was happy to see him healthy and thriving.

Before she pulled away, he held her by the shoulder and whispered, "You know what you need to do to live the life you want."

She stood back up, staring at her dad and nodded.

"Hey, want to go get a drink with me?" she asked Eva, who seemed like she was ready for a break.

Eva nodded.

"We'll be right back!" Sky said, with a few obviously doubting that.

They headed for the bar and waited for the bartender to finish with another customer.

"You guys were amazing!" It was Keith, sitting at the bar stool beside them.

Eva smiled politely. He'd been doing better to not be the worst guy in the room anymore and it meant a lot to see his attitude changing towards them.

"Thanks. I saw you in the crowd." Eva had come a long way from being in the background or living as a hermit, to speaking to her bully as if they never had a bad day shared between them.

He nodded and smiled, placing a ten-dollar bill on the counter and walking away once he was finished being served.

"Growth!" Sky said.

Eva nodded. "For a lot of people!"

Sky reached for Eva's hand and stepped closer. They were still in the same formal clothes they'd worn at the play, Eva's *Star Wars* tie standing out over her black button-up shirt. Sky absently reached in, lightly tugging it before looking up into Eva's eyes.

There was so much Sky needed to say but she had to do one thing first. So, she did. Her lips pressed against Eva's and her body melted into her. The kiss was soft and sweet. Sky continued to tug at Eva's tie and found herself moaning when arms enclosed her waist.

When their lips parted, Eva's eyes were focused on only her.

"I don't feel uncomfortable or scared when you're beside me. I can look around... see people watch... and think... I'm lucky. I have everything I need and want now and there is no reason I should hide anymore. I'm successful, I feel good in my own skin, I'm funny when I don't mean to be..."

Sky laughed.

Eva smiled and took a breath.

"I have someone who loves me, and I love them back. I want us to stay patient, and experience every moment we have, and cherish the moments we don't, feeling blessed that we can and will."

"It's funny you say that," Sky said, nervous to get her words out. She was still in Eva's caressed embrace. "Here's the thing. I thought I needed the big city to fulfill my dreams in the cosmetic and costume artist industry. But the truth is... I've always felt lonely out there, struggling for a purpose that didn't feel right. And being here... helping Chas with the play... it was the first time I felt like my passion was being fulfilled."

"What are you saying?" Eva asked.

"This sounds so lesbian of me, but I don't care. I would move back with or without you in my life. But the fact that I do have you... it makes me want to run back. I know what this is for me."

Eva nodded. "I would have come and tried to stay in the city at some point if you really wanted to live there," Eva admitted.

Sky laughed. "That would have given you a heart attack!"

"Probably, but you are worth it. All the years of fantasizing about a love that I could jump over mountains for and someone doing the same for me." Eva shrugged. "Here we are now!"

"I want to work with Chas again and build a career out here. And if a gig I want comes up in the city, I can drive the few hours needed to do it." Sky was sure of her future and how she wanted it to be. She couldn't picture any other way of living.

"I love you, Eva. I want… need… a future with you in it. As my partner. My best friend. One day, my wife. I want kids with you. I need to live in that house with you. And take walks to the creek with you. Make a real life together. All I need to know, is if that's something you want to pursue with me?"

Eva reached up and cupped Sky's cheek. She smiled, all the years of being alone vanishing. She leaned in, their noses brushing together and kissed Sky, before whispering, "Hell yeah!"

About the Author

Domina Alexandra is a native of Southern California and currently lives in Atlanta, GA but is planning her big cross-country journey back to good old Oregon. She is an author of inspiring queer female protagonists, authentic emotions and thrilling action scenes that mirror her past career as an EMT and in Law Enforcement. Not to mention finding unique places that inspire her fantasy universe. She grew up writing poetry as an outlet. In 2006, she joined a Live Theater program where she played many roles in a production of plays and musicals. During her four years of acting, she fell in love with writing monologues, screenplays, and all things storytelling. When Domina's not writing, or finding new things to explore, she's soaking her feet in the dirt to ground herself, creating her fitness entrepreneur path, running wild with her dog, Carson, and baking.

Other Titles Available From Triplicity Publishing

One Shot at Love by Domina Alexandra. Newly retired from the WNBA, 'Jazzy' Jazz Thomas moves back home in hopes of rebuilding a friendship she once lost. Tamara made the biggest mistake of her life pushing Jazz away and despite her fears, all she wants is a second chance. Never mind the fact that she's been in love with Jazz all these years. Jazz has spent the past fourteen years wondering why Tamara ended their friendship and she won't miss the opportunity to find out why. With nothing but time to rekindle their friendship, Tamara's secrets will come out, leaving Jazz with one question. Will they both leap forward and take their one shot at love, or will they cave under pressure?

A Fated Love (Rogue Series Book 2) by Domina Alexandra. Starting over is never easy, however, Karissa wouldn't have it any other way if it meant being with her fated mate, Danni, a lone wolf whose own journey has been met with a lot of curves, starting with Hansel, the witch wolf, who turned her at fifteen and habitually shows up uninvited. Living as rogues, all they wanted was time to figure out their future, but when young rogue shifters start to go missing it will be up to Karissa and Danni to find them. To make matters more sinister, a very old vampire might be the reason for the young shifters being snatched. It will take more than Karissa and Danni to unravel the truth and find the shifters before it's too late.

Fae and Moon Bound (Claim Series Book 4) by Domina Alexandra. Less than a year as a newly awakened werewolf and Omega, Bonnie's life has yet to be boring. Surviving rogue werewolves, ghouls, and a dangerous stalker should make Bonnie feel more confident in surviving the future, but then again, she lets herself be captured to protect her pack and family. One thing Bonnie had not anticipated was being reunited with someone from her past.

A Rogue's Redemption (Rogue Series Book 1) by Domina Alexandra. Forcibly turned into a werewolf, Danni's life has been trapped by her creator for years, until the Sentinel of a Sacramento pack finds her in a fighting pit next to a couple dead wolves. As the pack's Sentinel, Karissa doesn't get much respect for her position. When she busts an illegal fighting pit in her territory and finds a werewolf with a power far greater than she's ever seen, she realizes she's not only found her one true mate, but she'll have her role as Sentinel questioned now more than ever.

New Beginnings by Graysen Morgen. Captain Tristan Malloy has dedicated her life to the Army and takes her job very seriously. When an unexpected situation arises back home, her world is upended. When the dust settles, she makes a choice that will change her life forever. Courtney Hewitt is a third generation Army helicopter pilot, who's been flying in and out of warzones until she gets sent to South America for a Special Forces Operation. The redeployment is a welcomed change of scenery, and the leader of the special forces team she's assigned to work with is an added bonus Courtney can't wait to cash in on, until the alluring captain abruptly kicks her to the curb, ending their secret, torrid affair. When Courtney follows her home on leave and discovers the reason, she must make a choice of her own. Everyone deserves a chance at a new beginning in this action-packed romance.

An Omega's Grief (Claimed Series Book 3) by Domina Alexandra. Bonnie's life is finally slowing down, but on a weekend getaway with her mate Rikki, things quickly turn sour when a human is killed right in front of them. Worse, Bonnie has a stalker with an unimaginable power, and if she doesn't confront this dangerous individual, it might cost her pack and friends their lives. With time against her, Bonnie will have to make her toughest decision yet.

Crossed Reins by Graysen Morgen. Barrel racing is Carly Rae Walsh's life, until it's ripped out from under her. With nothing to do and nothing to lose, she uses her years of horse whispering skills and intuition to train a troubled thoroughbred racehorse. Allison McKinley is a world class dressage rider who has stepped back from the spotlight to mourn the sudden death of her mother. The last thing she needs when she decides to start training again for competition, is her father's impulsive desire to own a racehorse, and his bizarre decision to choose a rodeo barrel racer as the trainer. The two women have nothing in common except horses, and even that's a stretch. Can they uncross the reins long enough to see what's happening between them?

Outside In by Breanna Hughes. Cali Evans is a survivor. Her life hasn't been easy, but her late father raised her to be smart, tough, and dependent only on herself and her wits. On the eve of her 21st birthday she meets Owen Bray - a beautiful and intriguing young doctor who equally frustrates and captivates Cali. That fateful meeting inspires Cali to make a better life for herself. The next day, hoping to make positive change, Cali hops a bus for the West Coast but never reaches her destination. Instead, she wakes up in an underground bunker with no recollection of how she got there. Upon her arrival, she learns that she's one of just forty survivors of a fast-spreading environmental toxin and that human life outside of the bunker has ceased to exist. Tired of the vague explanations and half-answers coming from the people in charge, Cali takes it upon herself to investigate the real reason why she's there and begins to uncover the sinister truth.

I Love You, Nora Whispered by Kathy L. Salt. Love in the time of horses and polio. England, 1948. Nora Lakes suffers from post Polio Syndrome and very low self-esteem. When her sister Martha manages to get her a job at Waterhouse Acre Stables, she can hardly believe it. She had never imagined that anyone would have employed her, damaged as she is. She also never imagined she would meet anybody like Katherine. Katherine Waterhouse was born with a silver spoon in her mouth. She has a mean streak and doesn't like people in general. What she does like, is horses. She wants to be a professional rider but growing up in a conservative house where her choices are limited by her sex, Katherine has always been trapped in her role as a woman. Nora and Katherine - two women with very different backgrounds, drawn to each other with an intensity neither of them is prepared for. Do they stand a chance?

Omega Rising (Claimed Series Book 2) by Domina Alexandra. A few months of peace. That was all Bonnie Collins was granted. New trouble has surfaced and go figure, this trouble came with a new pair of claws. When an unknown pack comes to town, Bonnie is forced to make tough decisions that will influence her packs future. Things only get harder when her mate is taken, leaving Bonnie in charge of a pack who still doesn't trust her. With chaos all around, it will be exactly what Bonnie needs to finally embrace what she has become. An Omega Rising. Book 2 of the *Claimed Series*.

Loose Ends by Joan L. Anderson. After her estranged sister is killed when she falls onto the subway tracks in Paris just as a train arrives, Allison goes to Paris to deal with her sister's body and collect her things. But, after talking to the police about the accident and viewing the subway surveillance video, something seems odd about her death. When Allison's hotel room in Paris is broken into with only a few things taken, but not any money or credit cards, she begins to wonder if it really was an accident that killed her sister, or if it was murder. Once Allison returns to Washington, D.C. to handle her sister's affairs, she soon realizes that her sister had been living a secret life and wasn't the person she had always thought she was. As troubling things begin to happen to Allison in D.C., she starts wondering if she will be the next person to die.

Real Love by Graysen Morgen. Leigh Myer is a trauma nurse practitioner who is not happy going through the motions of her daily life. When a friend offers up her mountain cabin for a relaxing vacation, Leigh packs her bags. She's never been to the mountains and certainly never in heavy snow. A chance meeting with a fish and wildlife officer turns her idea of a quiet, relaxing vacation…upside down. Camden Gorely loves her job and loves the mountain she works and lives on even more. She's tired of having flings with vacationers who visit for days or weeks at a time, until she meets the elusive nurse from the city. Can Leigh stop running from her past and allow real love into her heart?

Love Undercover by Domina Alexandra. Remi Stone never expected to get the opportunity to work undercover for narcotics. But, when the chance arrives, she takes it. With drugs coursing through a high school, Remi has only until the end of the school year to find the suspects responsible. Undercover, Remi plays her role, moving one step further into the drug industry. She never thought she'd be moving one step closer to the woman who would change her life and take hold of her heart. There is just one issue. Remi Stone is undercover as an eighteen-year-old high school senior. And the woman she can't seem to ignore is her History teacher. There will be a lot of challenges along the way, including one that could cost Remi her life and her heart.

Playing the Game by Graysen Morgen. Randi Rojas is a professional soccer player who seemingly has it all, a successful career, a long-term girlfriend, a loving family, and a great group of friends…until a chance meeting with an attractive woman sends her way offside, and into a whole new game. Berkley Ward lives her life to the extreme, spending her days either in the gym or four-wheeling in the woods, and her nights patrolling the streets as an officer. Affairs with taken women are easy, but after years of playing games, she's finished...until she meets a beautiful woman and a game she can't resist. Both women play a dangerously seductive game of cat and mouse, teetering on the edge of friendship and affair.

Rebel Sweetheart by Sydney Canyon. When a headstrong, country music superstar starts getting threatening letters while on tour, her manager has no other choice but to hire someone to investigate the threats and keep her safe. Haley Nielsen is as stubborn as it gets. She does things her way, and her way only. The last thing she needs or wants is a babysitter following her every move and controlling everything she does. Shane Crowley isn't your typical private investigator, or bodyguard, for that matter. She's a former U.S. Deputy Marshal with a lot of experience, and an all or nothing attitude. Tempers flare and the energy burns red hot between the two women as they spend weeks together cooped up on Haley's tour bus, traveling the country. Will they stop resisting each other long enough to see eye to eye? Or will the letter writer make good on his threats?

A Tale of Spiders and Canned Soup by Kathy L. Salt. Living on your own can be hard, but even more so when you're dealing with haphephobia; the death of a twin sister; and a crush on your teacher. Mika is still in contact with her foster family who homes the loves of her life, three young children she would do anything for, when she begins attending University of Aberdeen and meets Pauline, an Australian that teaches Viking history. Neither woman is used to breaking the rules, and their way to each other is a hard one, especially when Mika vows to get custody of the children, whether she is ready to be a parent or not. *A story* *about growing up. A story about dealing with grief. A story about Mika and Pauline.*

A Night Claimed (Claimed Series Book 1) by Domina Alexandra. Bonnie Collins had plans. And being a werewolf wasn't one of them. Attacked by a rogue who was out to claim her and facing what she now has no choice of becoming, Bonnie can't let go of her human life as a Paramedic. The last thing Bonnie needs is more challenges. However, Rikki, the Alpha of Mill City will be just that. Finding her to be possessive and ruling, Bonnie begins challenging the Alpha's every breath. Finding out her attack was no accident only makes her more angry at the situation. A group of rogues are out to get her. With no clue why, Bonnie has no choice but to seek help from the alluring Alpha and her pack, accepting the new world she was forced into.

Stunted by Breanna Hughes. Professional stuntwoman Jessie Knight takes her job very seriously and although she works in the entertainment industry, she has zero desire for fame or notoriety. She also has a very strict no-dating policy when it comes to coworkers. That is, until she meets famous actress Elliot Chase on the set of her new film. The adrenaline rush of the stunts is nothing compared to the sparks that fly between them. After a passionate night together, a sex tape is leaked that sends Jessie and Elliot's private and professional lives into a spiral. Will the fallout be too much for them to last? Or will they find a way out of the mess together?

Mission Compromised by Graysen Morgen. Natalia Moreno is thrilled when she arrives in Fiji for a relaxing vacation. However, she soon discovers the overwater bungalow she's staying in has been double booked for the entire stay, and the resort is full. Annoyed and frustrated, she has no other choice but to share her hut with a stranger. Christian Garnier is sent to Fiji for what she refers to as a working vacation, until she finds out she has an ornery roommate for the next two weeks who is dead set on making her job twice as hard. Soon, all hell breaks loose, and the two women are sent around the world on a wild goose chase.

Stargazing by Kathy L. Salt. Lissa stared open-mouthed at the GIF that played over and over on the screen in front of her. Heat flushed to her face, igniting her skin. Her heart started pounding in her chest. *Stupid internet, it should really come with a warning label.* She's never been interested in relationships or sex and as the years have gone by she has retreated more and more into her work. Everything changes when she meets Star, a porn actress with a heart of gold and a troubled childhood. *They say that opposites attract, but how much of that is true? What chance do they have when one of them is a virgin and the other one star in pornography?*

I Belong with Her by Domina Alexandra. Tajel Pierce loves the thrill of being a paramedic. Every call she goes on gives her a rush. She makes no time for a personal life. No one can ruin her love for her career. Then there is Arianna Castaldi, who just transferred to her new paramedic position in a whole new state. All she needs is a new start without any distractions. Arianna and Tajel's relationship doesn't start off perfect. Embarrassed of the one-night stand Arianna believes she had with Tajel, she wants to pretend they never met and make their relationship strictly business. The only choice they have to keep from strangling each other is to go from denying their feelings to accepting them as they work through intense 911 calls.

Nautical Delights by S. L. Gape. Lady Elizabeth Barrington has spent her entire life trying to please her family; constantly opting for a quiet life, she utilises her profession as a doctor to keep out of her families' clutches; bar the annual two-week Caribbean private cruise, where there is simply no budge. Confined to two weeks on board the *Iconica* super yacht, she intends on keeping her head down and enjoying as much of the holiday as she can, whilst keeping her family at arm's length. Until a crew member catches her eye.

Worlds Apart by S.L. Gape. Hollywood A-lister Heidi Spencer-Brady is everything you'd expect of an Idol. Loved by all, the British Beauty is graceful, talented, humble and so far removed from the 'typical' LA scene. When her husband's infidelity with his new 'leading lady' is leaked, Dawn, Heidi's best friend and manager, goes all out to protect her. She arranges for Heidi to go back to the UK and stay on her cousins farm they had visited as children, much to the disappointment of the animal fearing Heidi.

Castor Valley (Law & Order Series Book 2) by Graysen Morgen. Jessie Henry is torn when she reads about the capture of the Doyle brothers, two young men who were part of her old gang. Unable to let them hang for a crime she's sure they didn't commit, Jessie leaves her wife and the Town of Boone Creek behind and sets out on a journey back to the one place she thought she'd never see again, *Castor Valley*. Ellie Henry watches the love of her life leave, not knowing if she will ever return. When she gets an odd telegram, nearly a week later, she fears Jessie is in trouble. With no other choice, she goes to the one person who can help her.

Fight to the Top by S. L. Gape. Georgia is a forty-year-old, single, Area Director from Manchester, UK who is all work and definitely no play. Having no time to socialise or spend time with her family she prides herself on being fit and well-polished. Erika is an Area Director for the same company, but in the United States. Whilst she is concentrating so heavily on the promotion she has been fighting for, she's starting to feel like her life outside of work is falling apart. The two women are exceptionally different, and worlds apart. Both of their lives are turned upside down when their jobs are snatched from under their noses, and they are suddenly faced with being thrown together by their bosses for one last major project...in Texas.

Boone Creek (Law & Order Series Book 1) by Graysen Morgen. Jessie Henry is looking for a new life. She's unknown in the town of Boone Creek when she arrives and wants to keep it that way. When she's offered the job of Town Marshal, she takes it, believing that protecting others and upholding the law is the penance for her past. Ellie Fray is a widowed, shopkeeper. She generally keeps to herself, but the mysterious new Town Marshal both intrigues and infuriates her. She believes the last thing the town needs is someone stirring up trouble with the outlaws who have taken over.

Witness by Joan L. Anderson. Becca and Kate have lived together for eight years and have always spent their vacation in a tropical paradise, lying on a beach. This year, Becca wanted to try something different: a seven day, 65-mile hike in the beautiful Cascade Mountains of Washington state. Their peaceful vacation turns to horror when they stumble upon a brutal murder taking place in the back country.

Too Soon by S.L. Gape. Brooke is a twenty-nine-year-old detective from Oxford, who has her life pretty much planned out until her boss and partner of nine years, Maria, tells her their relationship is over. When Brooke finds out the truth, that Maria cheated on her with their best friend Paula, she decides to get her life back on track by getting away for six weeks in Anglesey, North Wales. Chloe, a thirty-three-year-old artist and art director, owns a log cabin on Anglesey where she spends each weekend painting and surfing. After returning from a surf, she stumbles upon the somewhat uptight and enigmatic Brooke.

Never Quit (Never Series Book 2) by Graysen Morgen. Two years after stepping away from the action as a Coast Guard Rescue Swimmer to become an instructor, Finley finds herself in charge of the most difficult class of cadets she's ever faced, while also juggling the taxing demands of having a home life with her partner Nicole, and their fifteen-year-old daughter. Jordy Ross gave up everything, dropping out of college, and leaving her family behind, to join the Coast Guard and become a rescue swimmer cadet. The extreme training tests her fitness level, pushing her mentally and physically further than she's ever been in her life, but it's the aggressive competition between her and another female cadet that proves to be the most challenging.

Never Let Go (Never Series Book 1) by Graysen Morgen. For Coast Guard Rescue Swimmer, Finley Morris, life is good. She loves her job, is well respected by her peers, and has been given an opportunity to take her career to the next level. The only thing missing is the love of her life, who walked out, taking their daughter with her, seven years earlier. When Finley gets a call from her ex, saying their teenage daughter is coming to spend the summer with her, she's floored. While spending more time with her daughter, whom she doesn't get to see often, and learning to be a full-time parent, Finley quickly realizes she has not, and will never, let go of what is important.

Pursuit by Joan L. Anderson. Claire is a workaholic attorney who flies to Paris to lick her wounds after being dumped by her girlfriend of seventeen years. On the plane she chats with the young woman sitting next to her, and when they land the woman is inexplicably detained in Customs. Claire is surprised when she later runs into the woman in the city. They agree to meet for breakfast the next morning, but when the woman doesn't show up Claire goes to her hotel and makes a horrifying discovery. She soon finds herself ensnared in a web of intrigue and international terrorism, becoming the target of a high stakes game of cat and mouse through the streets of Paris.

Wrecked by Sydney Canyon. To most people, the *Duchess* is a myth formed by old pirate's tales, but to Reid Cavanaugh, a Caribbean island bum and one of the best divers and treasure hunters in the world, it's a real, seventeenth century pirate ship—the holy grail of underwater treasure hunting. Reid uses the same cunning tactics she always has before setting out to find the lost ship. However, she is forced to bring her business partner's daughter along as collateral this time because he doesn't trust her. Neither woman is thrilled but being cooped up on a small dive boat for days forces them to get know each other quickly.

Arson by Austen Thorne. Madison Drake is a detective for the Stetson Beach Police Department. The last thing she wants to do is show a new detective the ropes, especially when a fire investigation becomes arson to cover up a murder. Madison butts heads with Tara, her trainee, deals with sarcasm from Nic, her ex-girlfriend who is a patrol officer, and finds calm in the chaos of police work with Jamie, her best friend who is the county medical examiner. Arson is the first of many in a series of novella episodes surrounding the fictional Stetson Beach Police Department and Detective Madison Drake.

***Mommies (Bridal Series Book 3)* by Graysen Morgen.** Britton and her wife Daphne have been married for a year and a half and are happy with their life, until Britton's mother hounds her to find out why her sister Bridget hasn't decided to have children yet. This prompts Daphne to bring up the big subject of having kids of their own with Britton. Britton hadn't really thought much about having kids, but her love for Daphne makes her see life and their future together in a whole new way when they decide to become mommies.

Rapture & Rogue by Sydney Canyon. Taren Rauley is happy and in a good relationship, until the one person she thought she'd never see again comes back into her life. She struggles to keep the past from colliding with the present as old feelings she thought were dead and gone, begin to haunt her. In college, Gianna Revisi was a mastermind, ring-leading, crime boss. Now, she has a great life and spends her time running Rapture and Rogue, the two establishments she built from the ground up. The last person she ever expects to see walk into one of them, is the girl who walked out on her, breaking her heart five years ago.

Second Chance by Sydney Canyon. After an attack on her convoy, Marine Corps Staff Sergeant, Darien Hollister, must learn to live without her sight. When an experimental procedure allows her to see again, Darien is torn, knowing someone had to die in order for this to happen. She embarks on a journey to personally thank the donor's family but is too stunned to tell them the truth. Mixed emotions stir inside of her as she slowly gets to the know the people that feel like so much more than strangers to her. When the truth finally comes out, Darien walks away, taking the second chance that she's been given to go back to the only life she's ever known, but she's not the only one with a second chance at life.

Meant to Be by Graysen Morgen. Brandt is about to walk down the aisle with her girlfriend, when an unexpected chain of events turns her world upside down, causing her to question the last three years of her life. A chance encounter sparks a mix of rage and excitement that she has never felt before. Summer is living life and

following her dreams, all the while, harboring a huge secret that could ruin her career. She believes that some things are better kept in the dark, until she has her third run-in with a woman she had hoped to never see again, and gives into temptation. Brandt and Summer start believing everything happens for a reason as they learn the true meaning of meant to be.

Coming Home by Graysen Morgen. After tragedy derails TJ Abernathy's life, she packs up her three-year-old son and heads back to Pennsylvania to live with her grandmother on the family farm. TJ picks back up where she left off eight years earlier, tending to the fruit and nut tree orchard, while learning her grandmother's secret trade. Soon, TJ's high school sweetheart and the same girl who broke her heart, comes back into her life, threatening to steal it away once again. As the weeks turn into months and tragedy strikes again, TJ realizes coming home was the best thing she could've ever done.

Special Assignment by Austen Thorne. Secret Service Agent Parker Meeks has her hands full when she gets her new assignment, protecting a Congressman's teenage daughter, who has had threats made on her life and been whisked away to a Christian boarding school under an alias to finish out her senior year. Parker is fine with the assignment, until she finds out she has to go undercover as a Canon Priest. The last thing Parker expects to find is a beautiful, art history teacher, who is intrigued by her in more ways than one.

Miracle at Christmas by Sydney Canyon. A Modern Twist on the Classic Scrooge Story. Dylan is a power-hungry lawyer who pushed away everything good in her life to become the best defense attorney in the, often winning the worst cases and keeping anyone with enough money out of jail. She's visited on Christmas Eve by her deceased law partner, who threatens her with a life in hell like his own, if she doesn't change her path. During the course of the night, she is taken on a journey through her past, present, and future with three very different spirits.

Bella Vita by Sydney Canyon. Brady is the First Officer of the crew on the Bella Vita, a luxury charter yacht in the Caribbean. She enjoys the laidback island lifestyle, and is accustomed to high profile guests, but when a U.S. Senator charters the yacht as a gift to his beautiful twin daughters who have just graduated from college and a few of their friends, she literally has her hands full.

Brides (Bridal Series Book 2) by Graysen Morgen. Britton Prescott is dating the love of her life, Daphne Attwood, after a few tumultuous events that happened to unravel at her sister's wedding reception, seven months earlier. She's happy with the way things are, but immense pressure from her family and friends to take the next step, nearly sends her back to the single life. The idea of a long engagement and simple wedding are thrown out the window, as both families take over, rushing Britton and Daphne to the altar in a matter of weeks.

Cypress Lake by Graysen Morgen. The small town of Cypress Lake is rocked when one murder after another happens. Dani Ricketts, the Chief Deputy for the Cypress Lake Sheriff's Office, realizes the murders are linked. She's surprised when the girl that broke her heart in high school has not only returned home, but she's also Dani's only suspect. Kristen Malone has come back to Cypress Lake to put the past behind her so that she can move on with her life. Seeing Dani Ricketts again throws her off-guard, nearly derailing her plans to finally rid herself and her family of Cypress Lake.

Crashing Waves by Graysen Morgen. After a tragic accident, Pro Surfer, Rory Eden, spends her days hiding in the surf and snowboard manufacturing company that she built from the ground up, while living her life as a shell of the person that she once was. Rory's world is turned upside down when a young surfer pursues her, asking for the one thing she can't do. Adler Troy and Dr. Cason Macauley from Graysen Morgen's bestselling novel: *Falling Snow*, make an appearance in this romantic adventure about life, love, and letting go.

Bridesmaid of Honor (Bridal Series Book 1) by Graysen Morgen. Britton Prescott's best friend is getting married and she's the maid of honor. As if that isn't enough to deal with, Britton's sister announces she's getting married in the same month and her maid of honor is her best friend Daphne, the same woman who has tormented Britton for years. Britton has to suck it up and play nice, instead of scratching her eyes out, because she and Daphne are in both weddings. Everyone is counting on them to behave like adults.

Falling Snow by Graysen Morgen. Dr. Cason Macauley, a high-speed trauma surgeon from Denver meets Adler Troy, a professional snowboarder, and sparks fly. The last thing Cason wants is a relationship and Adler doesn't realize what's right in front of her until it's gone, but will it be too late?

Fate vs. Destiny by Graysen Morgen. Logan Greer devotes her life to investigating plane crashes for the National Transportation Safety Board. Brooke McCabe is an investigator with the Federal Aviation Association who literally flies by the seat of her pants. When Logan gets tangled in head games with both women will she choose fate or destiny?

Just Me by Graysen Morgen. Wild child Ian Wiley has to grow up and take the reins of the hundred-year-old family business when tragedy strikes. Cassidy Harland is a little surprised that she came within an inch of picking up a gorgeous stranger in a bar and is shocked to find out that stranger is the new head of her company.

Love Loss Revenge by Graysen Morgen. Rian Casey is an FBI Agent working the biggest case of her career and madly in love with her girlfriend. Her world is turned upside when tragedy strikes. Heartbroken, she tries to rebuild her life. When she discovers the truth behind what really happened that awful night, she decides justice isn't good enough, and vows revenge on everyone involved.

Natural Instinct by Graysen Morgen. Chandler Scott is a Marine Biologist who keeps her private life private. Corey Joslen is intrigued by Chandler from the moment she meets her. Chandler is forced to finally open her life up to Corey. It backfires in Corey's face and sends her running. Will either woman learn to trust her natural instinct?

Secluded Heart by Graysen Morgen. Chase Leery is an overworked cardiac surgeon with a group of best friends that have an opinion and a reason for everything. When she meets a new artist named Remy Sheridan at her best friend's art gallery she is captivated by the reclusive woman. When Chase finds out why Remy is so sheltered will she put her career on the line to help her or is it too difficult to love someone with a secluded heart?

In Love, at War by Graysen Morgen. Charley Hayes is in the Army Air Force and stationed at Ford Island in Pearl Harbor. She is the commanding officer of her own female-only service squadron and doing the one thing she loves most, repairing airplanes. Life is good for Charley, until the day she finds herself falling in love while fighting for her life as her country is thrown haphazardly into World War II. Can she survive being in love and at war?

Fast Pitch by Graysen Morgen. Graham Cahill is a senior in college and the catcher and captain of the softball team. Despite being an all-star pitcher, Bailey Michaels is young and arrogant. Graham and Bailey are forced to get to know each other off the field in order to learn to work together on the field. Will the extra time pay off or will it drive a nail through the team?

Submerged by Graysen Morgen. Assistant District Attorney Layne Carmichael had no idea that the sexy woman she took home from a local bar for a one-night stand would turn out to be someone she would be prosecuting months later. Scooter is a Naval Officer on a submarine who changes women like she changes uniforms.

When she is accused of a heinous crime, she is shocked to see her latest conquest sitting across from her as the prosecuting attorney.

Vow of Solitude by Austen Thorne. Detective Jordan Denali is in a fight for her life against the ghosts from her past and a Serial Killer taunting her with his every move. She lives a life of solitude and plans to keep it that way. When Callie Marceau, a curious Medical Examiner, decides she wants in on the biggest case of her career, as well as Jordan's life, Jordan is powerless to stop her.

Igniting Temptation by Sydney Canyon. Mackenzie Trotter is the Head of Pediatrics at the local hospital. Her life takes a rather unexpected turn when she meets a flirtatious, beautiful fire fighter. Both women soon discover it doesn't take much to ignite temptation.

One Night by Sydney Canyon. While on a business trip, Caylen Jarrett spends an amazing night with a beautiful stripper. Months later, she is shocked and confused when that same woman re-enters her life. The fact that this stranger could destroy her career doesn't bother her. C.J. is more terrified of the feelings this woman stirs in her. Could she have fallen in love in one night and not even known it?

Fine by Sydney Canyon. Collin Anderson hides behind a façade, pretending everything is fine. Her workaholic wife and best friend are both oblivious as she goes on an emotional journey, battling a potentially hereditary disease that her mother has been diagnosed with. The only person who knows what is really going on, is Collin's doctor. The same doctor, who is an acquaintance that she's always been attracted to, and who has a partner of her own.

Shadow's Eyes by Sydney Canyon. Tyler McCain is the owner of a large ranch that breeds and sells different types of horses. She isn't exactly thrilled when a Hollywood movie producer shows up wanting to film his latest movie on her property. Reegan Delsol is an up-and-coming actress who has everything going for her when she lands the lead role in a new film, but there one small problem that could blow the entire picture.

Light Reading: A Collection of Novellas by Sydney Canyon. Four of Sydney Canyon's novellas together in one book, including the bestsellers Shadow's Eyes and One Night.

Visit us at www.tri-pub.com